S0-BMU-917

MOUSETRAPS

MOUSETRAPS

PAT SCHMATZ

Carolrhoda Books • Minneapolis • New York

So many people have helped me through the various drafts of this book, with information, inspiration, and detailed feedback. Many thanks to Susan Alborell, Linda Carvel, Eunice Charlton, Kate DiCamillo, Karen Dodson, the Elsberry Family, Catherine Friend, the Hayward Group (in and out of Hayward), Bob Hofer, the Legal Aid Society of Minneapolis, Mary Winston Marrow, Maggie Moris, the Monday Night Group at JRT's house, Kathy Pennington, Marsha Qualey, Jane St. Anthony, Jeff Schmatz, Ruth Schmatz, Tim Spencer, Matt Stevens, Robin Stevenson, Gwenyth Swain, Kim Swineheart, Jane Resh Thomas, and Karen Thompson.

Special thanks to Bill Hauser for the manifestation of Maxie's art, and to designer Danielle Carnito for her talented hand in the visuals. Also to Mat DeFiler, who worked with me to clarify the concept of linking text with graphics.

I'm very grateful to my agent, Andrea Cascardi, for seeing this story through its many changes; also to my editor, Shannon Barefield, for her clear vision and guidance.

—P.S.

Carolrhoda Books
A division of Lerner Publishing Group, Inc.
241 First Avenue North
Minneapolis, MN 55401 U.S.A.

Website address: www.lernerbooks.com

Library of Congress Cataloging-in-Publication Data

Schmatz, Pat.
      Mousetraps / by Pat Schmatz ; illustrations by Bill Hauser.
          p.   cm.
      Summary: When Maxie's best friend from elementary school returns years later
      after a horrible act of violence against him, Maxie feels guilty about how she treated
      him and conflicted over whether or not she wants to befriend him again.
          ISBN 978-0-8225-8657-9 (trade hardcover : alk. paper)
      [1. Bullying—Fiction. 2. Peer pressure—Fiction. 3. Identity—Fiction. 4.
High schools—Fiction. 5. Schools—Fiction. 6. Interpersonal relations—Fiction. 7.
Homosexuality—Fiction.] I. Hauser, Bill, ill. II. Title.
      PZ7.S34734Mo 2008
      [Fic]—dc22

                                                                          2008001186

Manufactured in the United States of America
1 2 3 4 5 6 – BP – 13 12 11 10 09 08

FOR
LISA ANN,
MERRY,
AND NORA J.

CHAPTER 1

"Nash, Roderick."

The name flew out of the past and into chemistry roll call on the first day of my junior year.

"It's Rick."

I whipped around, searching faces. A tall, thin boy with a whopping case of first-day acne looked right at me. Roddy. Roddy Nash. My best friend in elementary school. I'd never have recognized him, not by voice or looks. He turned up one side of his mouth and nodded. He'd probably been watching me since Ms. Patterson had called "Hawke, Maxie." I gave him a little wave and faced front.

I opened my notebook and drew a quick sketch of Roddy. Next to that I drew the guy I'd just seen.

He'd almost grown into his ears. When class ended,

I gathered my books and turned to say hi, but he'd already left out the back door. I went out that way too and looked up and down the crowded hallway, but he was long gone.

After school, I lay on my bedroom floor with my sketchbook open, remembering the day in fourth grade when Roddy and I started Nash & Hawke, Ink. He'd shown me a complicated diagram of gadgets and machines and wheels and cogs. It was a mess, like Charlie Brown's kite string tangle in *Peanuts* cartoons, where you couldn't possibly follow it from one end to the other.

"What's that thing?" I asked, pointing to one of the little things on either edge of the diagram.

"That's the mouse."

"Mouse?" I said. "That's not a mouse. Here, this is a mouse."

"Oh, hey, that's great, Maxie! Can you draw another one here? Midway through the trap? Look, this is the part where he falls down the chute, see…"

And we were off. He designed. I drew, and added remarks and exclamations from the surprised mouse. Rick invented newer and more complicated mousetraps through fourth and fifth grade, sloppy diagrams in ink with blotches and scratch-outs. Then he'd turn them over to me to draw. We worked out the details walking to and from school. Neighborhood kids used to sing that "Maxie and Roddy sittin' in a tree, k-i-s-s-i-n-g" song but back then it didn't bother me. I was busy.

I wrote "Nash & Hawke, Ink" across the top of the page and gave it a shot, just for old time's sake.

My cell phone started singing from the pocket of my backpack. I dug it out and flipped it open. My cousin Sean's number showed up on the screen. He was a senior, and he had left school at noon to go to his two classes at the university.

"Hey Max, guess who I saw in the parking lot on my way out?"

"Roddy Nash," I said, sitting back down on the floor.

"Oh, you saw him too," said Sean through the crunchy thing he was eating.

"Yeah, he's in my chemistry class. He's going by Rick now. Did you talk to him?"

"Nope," said Sean. "I bumped into him in the hall, but he acted like he didn't know me. Took one look and hoofed in the other direction."

"Maybe he didn't recognize you? You've changed a lot since he left."

"No, he knew it was me. I could see it on his face."

"Hm. Well, he didn't stick around to talk to me either," I said. "Speaking of changing, he doesn't look much like a Roddy anymore."

"That's no lie, he must be six-foot-four at least. He was about four-foot-nothing in seventh grade."

"I can't believe he came back," I said.

"Yeah, me neither. Talk about a blast from the past."

We were both quiet a moment, feeling that blast. It was something I'd managed not to think about for a long time.

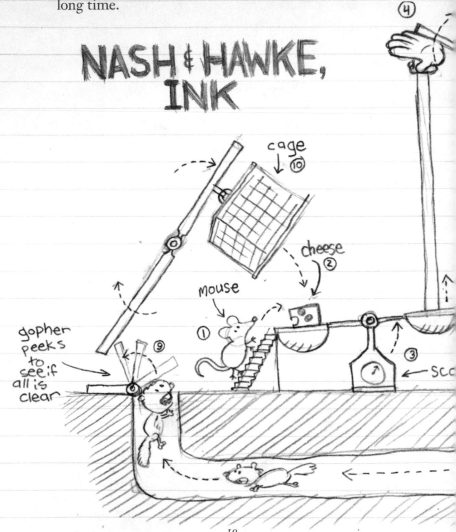

NASH & HAWKE, INK

"Hey, how's college?" I asked.

"So far so good," he said. "The theater class is gonna be cake, but the playwriting looks tough. Oh hey, I've got another call. Talk to you later."

He hung up. I put the phone down and looked at my drawing. Good mouse. Cute gopher. Stupid trap. It'd never work. I ripped it out, crumpled it, and tossed it into recycling.

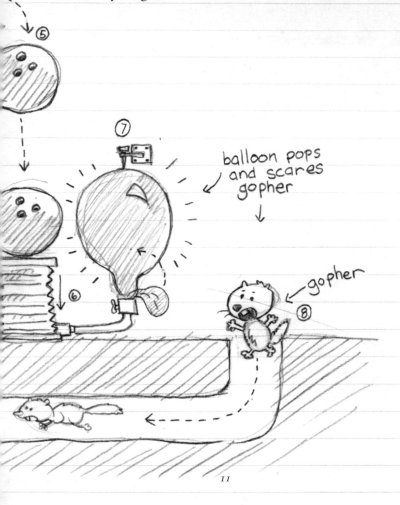

balloon pops and scares gopher

gopher

Next day I got to school early and sat at a table in the far corner of the Commons. I pulled out my sketchpad and looked around. We went to a big public high school, with middle schools from all over the city pouring into it. A hacky-sack circle started up nearby and I watched, getting the feel of the motion. I picked up my pencil, but I hadn't even gotten the first line on paper when my best friend, Tay Leighton, came up behind me and dropped her books on the table.

"Did you do the English assignment last night? Hey, can I have a piece of paper?"

I ripped one out of my notebook, and Tay started scrawling in her big sloppy script, her shaggy dark hair hanging over the paper. She wrote quickly, one paragraph after another, and finished with a flourish.

"Are you going to hand it in like that?" I asked.

"He didn't say it had to be typed," she said. "Not everyone has a computer at home, you know."

"Yeah, but you do."

"He doesn't know that." She grinned.

"Did you go skating last night?" I asked. "I tried calling you twice."

"Yeah, I met Brett at the rink downtown and kicked his ass all over the ice," she said. "He thinks he's gonna play varsity. His father's been putting false hopes in his little freshman head."

Brett's father was Tay's father, too, but she wouldn't call him that. He didn't count girls' hockey as a real sport—and since he'd moved out, she didn't count him as a real dad.

The bell rang and Tay and I headed up the stairs to get our books for English. At the top, we came around a corner just in time to see Jordan Feltz slam a pudgy freshman up against my row of lockers.

"When you speak to me, you call me *SIR*," he said. "Is that clear?"

"Shove it," the kid squeaked.

"Whoa," Tay said to me. "Who is that kid?"

Jordan thumped the heel of his hand on the kid's forehead. The kid's head banged against the locker, and Jordan grabbed his nose with a big paw and twisted hard. Tears came up in the kid's eyes.

"Better apologize for those bad manners, asswipe," said Jordan, playing for the crowd. "Or I'll take your nose right off your face and cram it down your throat."

"Teacher coming," someone yelled.

"You'd better watch it," Jordan said as he gave the kid a last shove. "I'm gonna remember you."

"Hey, is that Nash?" Tay nudged me and jerked her head to the left.

Rick was on the edge of the crowd, moving off in the other direction. I nodded and Tay stared after him.

"He sure got tall," she said.

"Yup."

I opened my locker and pulled out my books for English.

"Why'd he come back?"

"I don't know," I said. "I didn't ask."

"I thought maybe he'd have a broken nose or a scarred-up face or something," she said. "I mean, those guys who beat him up in seventh grade got five full days' suspension, remember? Jordan was in my English group and we had to do the final project without him."

I slammed my locker shut and headed for the stairs. Tay followed, still talking.

"Must've been because of his dad being rich, that those guys got in so much trouble," said Tay. "I mean, five days' suspension, you'd've thought they'd fractured his skull or something."

I started down the stairs, Tay behind me.

"He seems fine though," said Tay over my shoulder. "I guess they didn't do any permanent damage."

Tay had no idea. By the time she'd shown up at the start of seventh grade, I'd been ducking out of my friendship with Roddy for almost a year and hardly

talked to him. So when Sean told me about that day—
and made me promise not to tell—I'd kept the promise.
It was the only secret I'd ever kept from Tay.

The final bell rang, and we scurried down the hall
and slid into our seats just as Mr. Tolliver got up to close
the door. I pulled out my notebook and started to copy
the notes on the board.

When I got to chemistry fourth period, Rick was
watching the doorway, and he nodded as I came in. I
didn't really want to sit in the empty seat next to him,
but it would have looked weird to sit somewhere else. So
I smiled at him as I sat down, then opened my chemistry
book and waited for class to start.

Ms. Patterson told us to choose lab partners and
Rick looked at me. I couldn't think of anything to do
but nod, so then we were lab partners. We moved back
to lab stations to get oriented. We had to go through
the equipment and mark off the checklist to make sure it
was all there and sign that we were responsible for it.

The hum of chatter picked up in the room and
everything I could think of to say to him seemed
incredibly wrong, so we just did the work. We got
done before everyone else and then sat there on our lab
stools. I sketched little shapes on the table surface with
the eraser of my pencil, and Rick drummed his fingers
on his thigh. It was like someone had dropped a box of
silence around our lab station.

"You still draw?" Rick finally said, nodding at my
non-pictures on the table.

"Yup," I said.

"Remember Nash & Hawke, Ink?" he asked. "The traps?"

I nodded.

"We sure made some good ones," he said. "You drew the best mice. Remember, you said mine looked like squishy little snowmen with four stick legs."

Then we had some more silence, and pictures of middle school moved through my head. It wasn't like elementary school. Kids were all split up into different groups who didn't like each other.

The worst was Felicia Sorenson and her group. They called me a fag hag the first week of sixth grade,  when they saw me and Roddy walking home together. That got to me in a way the "kissin' in a tree" song never did, even though back then I wasn't sure what fag hag meant. That's when I'd started avoiding Roddy, making excuses about having too much homework or having to get home right away.

"You been here since freshman year?" Rick asked.

"Yup," I said.

"Got any ideas about after high school yet?" he asked.

"I don't know, college somewhere I guess. What about you?"

More silence. Rick drummed his fingers again. I wished for the bell to ring.

"Well, my father thinks he's going to make a soldier out of me."

"Really?" I laughed. "Why?"

"He's probably hoping I'll get killed. He'd rather have a nice folded-up American flag than have to look at my face. He says he won't pay anything for college unless I go into the service."

"Are you going to do it?"

"When pigs sprout fully feathered wings."

"Like that?" I asked him.

He took the picture and looked at it for a long time, nodding, and he smiled with one side of his face.

"You can still draw, Maxie Hawke," he said, handing it back to me.

"Keep it. If you want."

"No," he said. "It's too real. It might inspire me to run down to the recruiting station and enlist."

CHAPTER 3

Sean pulled up in front of the house that night in his little green MG and honked. I grabbed my sketchpad and a sweatshirt and pounded down the stairs and out the front door. The sun was still warm, but the breeze had a nip that we'd be feeling after dark. Sean rapped along with his tunes, dancing in his seat and telling it to the steering wheel. I opened the door and slid in.

Once Sean had made it out of middle-school hell, things had started looking up in a hurry. His mom, my Aunt Lisa, spent so much time at that school complaining about the bullying—for a while there Sean got it as bad as Roddy did—she might as well have had her own locker. She got put on probation at work for absenteeism, and Sean kept threatening to run away. They crawled through the last days of eighth grade, and then Uncles Max and Greg asked Lisa to let Sean live with them over the summer. They would help him figure out how to deal with school problems and Lisa could get her own life back on track.

The short-term fix turned into a long-term arrangement. The Unks were thrilled to have an insta-kid, Aunt Lisa got a break from the single-mom treadmill, and Sean got to bounce back and forth between two houses whenever he wanted. Extra bonus: he got the '63 MG from the Unks for his fifteenth birthday, a year before he could even drive it.

"What's the rush?" I asked as Sean rolled through a stop sign.

"I don't want to miss the pregame warmups," he said, punching the accelerator. We cornered off the side streets and onto the main drag with its traffic and billboards.

"So football has a whole new meaning for you now, huh?"

Sean grinned, his dimple showing. He was totally gone on Dexter Jones, our school's star running back. And topping my personal list of the unexpected, Dexter was into him too. They'd started hanging out together over the summer, and now Sean was dating the best-looking guy in school. They were keeping it quiet, though. Senior-year football season wasn't exactly prime for Dex to make any announcements or even be seen spending a lot of time with Sean McGinnis.

"So Rick Nash and I are lab partners," I said as we pulled up to a light.

"Really?"

"Uh-huh. Have you talked to him yet?"

"Nope. He won't even make eye contact with me."

"That's weird."

"I totally get it," said Sean. "If he wants to be Rick and forget Roddy ever happened, I say let him. I'm sure not going to get up in his face."

The light turned green and the car leapt ahead. Even though Sean hadn't changed his name, he'd changed everything else since those middle-school days. He'd grown, his baby fat shifted to muscle, and he got involved with theater the first summer he stayed with the Unks. Once he started high school, he always had a gang of drama girls hanging out with him, and they weren't shy about sticking up for him. After a few loud comments about closet cases being the biggest homophobes, even Jordan backed off and stopped yelling "You go girl!" at him all the time.

We came around the corner and into the lot. Sean skidded into a spot and turned the engine off.

"So you're lab partners now," he said. "How's he seem, anyway?"

"I don't know," I shrugged. "We had a kind of awkward conversation about future plans. He said his dad wants him to get killed in the army. You know, light talk."

"His dad's a piece of work," Sean shook his head. "If Rick ever came out, his dad would personally put his head on a flagpole. I only went over to his house once and that was enough."

Rick's scary dad →

"I know. He scared me even when he was acting nice."

"Yeah, well, imagine growing up with

that guy," said Sean.

I couldn't. Mr. Nash was so many light-years from my dad, it was hard to believe they were the same species. If I were to set up the human zoo, I'd put them in totally different sections.

We paid our money and headed for the bleachers. The band marched onto the field playing "Sergeant Pepper" as we climbed to the top row on the fifty-yard line and settled in. The sun sank behind the scoreboard and the team appeared on the edge of the field in a huge massed huddle, jogging in a tight unit and yelling in rhythm. The smells of hot dogs and nachos hit my nose. I hoped Tay remembered to bring me some food from work.

I glanced over at Sean, who had his eyes glued on Dexter. He leaned forward, his chin in his hands, his blue-green T-shirt spread across his broad back. Sean had the kind of wavy brown hair that always mussed itself just right. I didn't think it was fair that he got every single good look the family gene pool had to offer.

"How long do you think Dex can keep it under wraps?" I asked.

"Until football season is over, for sure," said Sean. "If those guys find out, they'll crucify him."

"Don't you think people are getting a clue?"

"We're careful at school," said Sean. "We hardly talk to each other. Besides, nobody wants Dex to be a fag, so they'll look the other way, you know? They'll work at not knowing. But then you've got Rick, who sure doesn't read queer to me, and they're all over him.

I heard someone call him a fag yesterday."

"Oh no, are they starting that again?

"Looks like. It's not so bad being called a faggot if you can just say yeah, so what."

"Really?" I asked.

"No," he said. "Really, it sucks either way. Hey, there's Tay."

He pointed to Tay at the bottom of the bleachers, still wearing her Taco Bell uniform. I loved the way she could get away with things like that—like she'd picked the uniform up at a thrift shop and worn it on purpose. She skipped up, grinning, the smell of onions and refried beans in a cloud around her, and passed me a bag full of Nachos Supreme. I set it between me and Sean, and we dug in.

That first day of seventh grade, when Tay showed up on roller blades with purple high tops hanging around her neck, I'd liked her right away because she looked like a cartoon. She was still one of my favorite people to draw, all long limbs and flowing movements.

"They look good," Tay said, nodding down at the field.

The guys ran drills, the receivers receiving, quarterbacks throwing, and the big guys roaring up off the line and pounding into each other. The assistant coach had Dex pulled off to the side, talking to him and smacking the side of his helmet while he jigged back and forth on his toes.

After the anthem, the teams lined up for kickoff and the game started. Watching Dexter run, that was pure pleasure whether you liked football or not. If he'd been bigger the stands would have been loaded with scouts. He was a little cyclone, spinning and bouncing off the bigger guys, ducking through holes and skittering downfield. Sometimes you just knew they had him, but then he spun or popped through and turned up on his feet, always running. He was on track to break the school rushing record, and all of that at five-foot-eight, 145 pounds.

Tay loved all sports and Sean was sucked in by Dexter's magic, so they were both riveted on the game. They kept up a running sportscast, and I found interesting people in the stands to draw.

Early in the fourth quarter we were behind by only four points. Dex caught a short pass and found a hole. He broke a tackle and shifted into a dead run downfield, and the lights went out.

Just like that. Totally dark.

The scoreboard went out, too. We all froze, waiting for the bang, or the flash, or whatever bad thing was going to happen. When the terrorists didn't bomb us and guns didn't go off, people started to murmur and make calls on their cells.

"What happened?" I whispered.

"I don't know," said Sean. "Power outage?"

"Maybe the other team's coach pulled the plug," said Tay. "Seeing Dex break out like that. Maybe they just want to sneak onto their bus and drive away."

A voice from the field yelled, "Attention, can I have your attention please?"

The crowd went quiet.

"If you'll just be patient, folks," the voice said, "we'll get the lights up here in a minute or two."

Actually, it took more like twenty minutes. We sat and waited, enjoying the unexpected. Like when the fire alarm goes off and everybody goes outside, and then you find out it was just a surprise drill and everything's really okay.

When the lights and scoreboard came back up, they didn't give our team the points for Dexter's touchdown. I don't see how anyone could think he wouldn't have made it, but they did the play over. The quarterback fumbled, we lost the ball, and then we lost the game.

We gave Tay a ride home, me sitting on her lap. She and Sean crabbed the whole way about getting our perfect season ruined before it even started.

"Like it's not obvious they got someone to cut the lights," said Tay. "They never could've beat us otherwise."

"I don't know," said Sean. "That's kind of a stretch—someone crawling around cutting wires during the game."

"Well, something fishy happened," she said as she

got out of the car. "And I bet we never do find out what. Call me tomorrow, Max?"

"Sure," I said.

We watched Tay fumble for her keys and let herself in the front door. Then Sean revved the engine and buzzed me home.

CHAPTER 4

Rick turned out to be a great lab partner. Not only did he understand the experiments and equations, but he could lead me through it all step by step, just like he used to do with his messy mousetraps. Without him, I'd have been lost in the first week. He figured things out and explained them to me, and I wrote up our lab reports. Nash & Hawke expanded to chemistry.

I did a good job of deleting Roddy memories from my Rick directory—or at least, keeping them buried away in some file that I never opened. Things were different now. I had a smart lab partner and might manage to get a B, and that was good. Like Sean said, it was probably best for everyone to pretend Roddy had never existed.

One Friday in October when I sat next to him, he didn't even look up when I said hi. He just kept scanning over the jumbled lines of writing in his notebook.

"Do we have a quiz today?" I asked, trying to remember how class had ended the day before.

He shook his head and kept studying. I watched

him for a bit, shrugged, took out my notebook, and opened to a clean page. Rick cleared
his throat and I glanced over at him. His cheeks were
flushed like maybe he was coming down with something. He met my glance and in that flash of a second
his eyes were open with something different, unguard-
ed. Young. He looked back down at his notes. Ms.
Patterson came in and started putting lab instructions
on the board, and the room settled down.

Patterson sent us back to the lab to do an experiment and I followed Rick to our station. I pulled up a
stool as he squatted to get supplies out of the cupboard.
He spread them all out on the lab table, stood, and
opened his book. As he flipped through pages without
looking up, he said, "So are you going to that dance?"

Sixth grade, just like that.

The tips of Rick's ears were so red I wondered if they actually hurt. I felt my own face get a little hot as I scanned the room for a way out. The moment stretched.

"Ah," I finally said. "I'm not really into the whole school dance thing. I went to a couple last year and they were boring. So I've decided to skip them."

"Oh," he said. "Sounds reasonable."

He put on his safety goggles without looking at me and handed me mine. Sixth-grade Roddy all over again. He knew that I knew that he knew that...

"You want to watch the thermometer or write numbers down?" he asked.

"I'll watch the thermometer."

I called out the numbers and he wrote them down. We finished the experiment, cleaned up our station, and went back to our table, where we both sat and wrote in silence. He was up and out of his chair at the first sound of the bell, taking waves of tension with him.

I leaned back in my chair, looked at the ceiling, and took what felt like my first full breath of the day. Then I picked up my books and went downstairs to find Tay. She was already in the lunch line, and I slid in behind her.

"Nightmare," I said. "Rick Nash just sort of asked me to the dance."

I picked up a tray and took a slice of pizza.

"Did you sort of tell him no?" asked Tay.

"Sort of. I told him I don't go to school dances."

"Well, that's sort of true," said Tay, picking up a brownie. "You haven't been to one this year."

"We haven't had one yet this year."

"Technicality," said Tay.

She grabbed two milks and balanced them on the edge of her tray. We headed for our favorite corner table, ignoring the sophomore girls at the other end who were whispering over a bag of baby carrots.

"Why is it always like that?" asked Tay. "The guys you like, they'd never ask, and meanwhile you get blindsided by some geeky guy you never would have thought of."

A frisbee came down over the balcony, and Tay snagged it before it crashed into her lunch. She threw it back up over the railing. Her friend Joe caught it and threw it to someone else.

"Anyway, good you ditched it," she said. "Hopefully he got the hint and you won't have to worry about him asking you out again."

"Who's asking you out?" said Dexter, coming up behind me. He set his tray down next to mine. "Who beat me to it?"

"Nobody," I said.

"Well good." He flashed me his glamour-boy smile. "Then I don't have any competition to fight off. Maxie, will you go to the dance with me?"

"What?"

"Come on, be my date," he said, taking half a piece of pizza in one bite. "It'll be very romantic and stuff."

"It'd be more romantic and stuff if you didn't ask her with your mouth full," said Tay. "What's the game?"

"Game is, we double date. You go with Sean, Maxie goes with me."

"What's in it for me?" I asked.

"You get a date with me," said Dexter, all flirty.

The way his green eyes and white teeth flashed against his dark skin, he looked like he'd just stepped off the screen. Full-on star power. Typical, the only way a guy like that would ask me out was so he could go with my cousin.

Jack Gorski, a linebacker, came by with his tray stacked high with food and slapped Dexter on the side of the head.

"Jonesy, you're supposed to be at the team table. Remember? We got that new play to go over."

"Just think about it, okay Maxie?" he said, getting up to follow Jack to the other side of the Commons.

"That is one pretty boy," Tay said, watching him go. "He's got all the best kind of DNA."

"All except the strand that makes him Sean's date instead of mine," I said. "Anyway, what do you think? Should we help the boys have their public night out?"

"It's not like I have offers lining up outside my door," said Tay, finishing off her pizza. "Except this kind of kills your 'I don't go to dances' excuse."

"Oh," I said, remembering. "Right."

"Well, you're not really going to the dance in the sense of, you know, 'going to the dance,'" said Tay. "It's just a favor to Sean."

She reached over and took my pizza crust, like she'd been doing since seventh grade.

"Another technicality?" I asked.

"Exactly," she nodded.

CHAPTER 5

Sunday was a stunning fall day, and my parents and I went out to the Grands' for family dinner. The Grands, my mom's parents, cooked almost every Sunday afternoon for the McGinnis clan and we usually went.

I rode in the back seat of our Toyota watching the trees go by. The maples were in their glory, with every shade from yellow to pink to orange to red and good enough to taste. The streets in our part of the city were lined with maples on the boulevards and an occasional yellow birch or blue spruce thrown in. If I had my way, October color would stretch out for six months of every year.

My parents tried to pull me into their conversation about some bad bill the state Senate was trying to pass, but I wouldn't bite. I watched the sky. The clouds were puffs of white and gray against a wide blue. Not just any blue, either. It was a musical blue with a taste and a smell and a feeling you could fall into if you stared deeply enough.

"Wonder what Grandma's got for dinner today," said Dad, breaking into my color world.

"Karen promised to bring pretzel jello this week," I said.

We pulled into the long driveway and passed under the friendly shade of the big oaks that stood on both sides.

"Have you been thinking about college options, riding so quietly back there?" asked Mom. "Planning for your future?"

"Ahhh, sure. That's what I've been doing."

"That's my daughter," Dad said, nodding and smiling.

"No, that's *my* daughter," said Mom. "Your daughter was looking out the window and thinking about absolutely nothing."

The car stopped, and I was out the door before the engine was off. I shot across the yard, through the front door, and into the kitchen before I even heard the other two car doors slam.

The smell of baking bread hit me when I walked in the front door. I loved arriving at the Grands' first, before the house filled with noise and I faded into the background. I liked to soak up Grandma and Grandpa on my own and pretend for a minute that I was their favorite.

Grandma pulled me tight when I came into the kitchen and kissed me firmly on the top of my head.

"Wassup, dude?" she asked.

"I'm not a dude, Grandma."

"You're all dude to me. Go kiss your grandpa and give his life some meaning."

I headed for the family room as my parents came in the front door.

"Hey Gramps."

"Hi Maximum."

I went over and gave him a kiss.

"Who's winning?" I asked.

"The Raiders," he said. "Can you believe it? They're winning, just like the old days."

"That's great, Grandpa."

"No, it's not. They're a bad-attitude team. Always have been, still are."

"Oh. Well then, that sucks, Grandpa."

"That's better."

I sat on the couch and looked at the orderly rows of school pictures Grandma kept on the wall. Mom was in the second row, right beneath Uncle Max, grinning from kindergarten picture to poofy-haired senior portrait. Us grandkids were a haphazard cluster on the opposite wall, with new pictures of different sizes coming in every year.

Laughter burst from the kitchen.

"Brought your folks along, did you?" asked Grandpa.

"Oh yeah, I let them come."

"How are they behaving? Do I need to take a belt to your mom?"

"Not this week," I said. "She's been pretty good, except for that thing where she keeps trying to make me be her."

Grandpa laughed. "No chance of that, now is there?"

Uncle Tommy stepped in, asking the score. The McGinnis men can fill a doorway, that's what Mom says. They all top six foot, with big shoulders and varying amounts of fat as they age. My nine-year-old cousin Jenny ducked under Tommy's arm for the obligatory Grandpa kiss. Uncle Jack appeared behind Tommy and put him in a stranglehold, starting a wrestling match and kicking off the general chaos.

I eventually drifted into the kitchen to scope out the food on the table.

"Maxie! My girl!" Uncle Max gave me a big squeeze. "I hear you and Tay are taking the boys to the dance. If that Sean doesn't do something really nice for you, let me know and I'll kick his stuff to the curb."

"I'll let you know," I said. "He's coming today, isn't he?"

"He's too important for the likes of us these days. Greg bribes him with the most exquisite meals and he still doesn't show up half the time. Is that Karen's famous pretzel jello I see?"

Uncle Greg moved up next to me as Max poked around the food on the table.

"So what do you think of this Dexter?" he asked me quietly.

"I don't know him very well," I said. "Haven't you met him yet?"

Greg shook his head.

"He's gorgeous, for whatever that's worth."

"So we've heard," said Greg. "Let's hope there's more to him than that."

"Out!" yelled Grandma. "Out of the kitchen. Quit picking at that food, Max. All of you out of here. I'll call you when it's ready."

I went out the front door, taking a break from the noise, and wandered down the driveway. The volume inside would amp up as the afternoon went on. I liked to move in and out, alternating between the circus in the house and the quiet open spaces of the farm.

I strolled over to the oaks and sat on the ground, pulling my sketchpad out of my back pocket. I moved back and forth against the rough bark, letting the tree scratch the itchy spot between my shoulder blades, and doodled. I sketched a network of branches, spreading and twining in and out as they stretched across the page. The leaves rustled overhead, and their shadows shifted and moved on the ground in front of me.

I set the sketchpad and pencil down and lay back against the tree trunk, scooting over so my face was in the shade. The leaves, still green but starting to dry, whispered as they moved against the deep blue.

Rick's going to find out, they said. He's going to find out you're going to the dance and it's going to hurt his feelings.

I reminded the leaves that I hadn't known about Dexter and Sean's idea when I told Rick I wasn't going. Besides, it'd be wrong to go out with him when I didn't want to.

You're ditching him again, just like middle school,

the leaves said. And because your crap isn't as crappy as everyone else's you pretend it's not crap. Don't you think he's had enough crap?

I'd been trying not to think about the crap that happened three and a half years ago, but sitting under the oaks brought it all back up again.

I'd looked all over the house for Sean on a hot Sunday in May before I finally spotted him behind one of these trees. He was huddled there, his arms wrapped around his knees, looking across the field.

"What are you doing out here?" I called. "It's almost dinnertime."

"Not hungry," he said.

I walked over and sat cross-legged, facing him. The grass was springy and still damp from the rain the night before.

"I tried to call you Friday night," I said. "Did your mom tell you?"

Sean nodded. I really looked at him for the first time and noticed his lashes were stuck-together spiky.

"Hey, are you okay?"

He shook his head and his lips shivered before he drew them in tight. He looked away from me.

"What's wrong?"

He shrugged. I tried not to roll my eyes because I could see he was really upset, but Sean was always one to pump a moment for whatever it was worth.

"Come on, Sean. Is it your mom? Is she freaking out again?"

Sean shook his head and then brought his eyes to

meet mine.

"Friday," he said. "Did you hear anything?"

"About the locker-room thing?" I asked. "You weren't there, were you? I thought it was the seventh graders."

"What'd you hear?" his voice was tight, low.

"Just that something happened after third period gym on Friday. A bunch of those guys from that hour were out the rest of the day, but nobody knew why."

"I promised not to tell anyone but it's making me crazy in my head, like if I don't say it out loud to someone who really gets it, then it's like it didn't happen, but it did, and I swear to God I'm never going back to that school."

"What happened?"

"Swear you won't tell anyone if I tell you. Not even your parents. Your mom would probably bring a lawsuit or something."

"Okay, I swear."

Sean picked up a twig and started peeling the bark off of it. He peeled the entire twig and then finally spoke.

"So you know it's bad in P.E., right?"

I knew. A few weeks earlier, Sean had gotten pantsed in front of everyone—girls too—while he was going for a rebound. The P.E. teacher, Mr. Weathers, told Aunt Lisa that Sean needed to have a little thicker skin, a better sense of humor.

"Tay thought somebody probably got beat up," I said.

Sean put his forehead down on his knees and rocked back and forth, shaking his head.

"Worse," he said.

"Worse?" I leaned in close so I could hear. "Worse what?"

"They hurt Roddy," said Sean, his voice breaking. "They messed him up bad."

"What do you mean, messed him up?" My stomach went tight.

"I'd come in just after the bell ending third period so I could get changed before everyone else got there, and the seventh graders were in the shower, all of them dressed but Roddy. I asked what was going on and Mike said they were going to butt-fuck him with a broom and if I wanted some I should get in line."

"What'd you do?" I asked through a dry mouth, although I didn't want to hear any more. Sean looked up at me, his breath shaking its way in and out and his face red and blotchy. He could barely get words out.

"I ran into Mr. Weathers' office and I'm screaming at him, hurry up, hurry up, and he took for-frickin-EVER, and by the time we got there..."

He dropped his head again.

I had about seven simultaneous movies running in my head and none of them were ones I should have been allowed to see.

"What, Sean? What happened?"

"Maxie, they ripped his balls. I think they were just screwing around, they didn't mean to but somebody slipped or pushed at the wrong time and—" He sobbed so hard his head bounced up and down.

"Oh my God. Is he going to be okay?"

"Okay?" Sean lifted his face, streaming tears and snot. "Okay? Are you crazy? How can he ever be okay?"

"Well, is he in the hospital or what?"

"I don't know. Nashes hushed it up. I have no idea if he's okay or dead or what. Nobody picked up when I called. Then later Mr. Nash called my mom and told her the best thing I can do is keep my mouth shut. If I try to tell they'll say it never happened. Call me a liar. But I can't go back to that school and act like it didn't happen, I can't, Maxie, I just can't."

I'd had no idea what to do, and I wished he'd never told me—or at least that I could forget he had. Rod didn't come back to school before summer break, and neither did any of the guys who'd been there, so things stayed hushed.

I'd decided to be extra nice to Roddy the next fall, not to say anything about what had happened, of course, but just go out of my way to say hi and be friendly, sort of make up for blowing him off in sixth grade. I never got the chance, though. Sean's letters got returned unopened, and by fall someone else was living in the Nashes' house.

"Hey Maxie!" Jenny yelled from the front stoop, jerking me back to the present. "What are you doing?"

I blinked hard and shook my head, chasing the pictures away. They were just as bad now as they'd been back then.

"Nothing!" I yelled back at her.

She ran across the yard and plopped down next to me. Three of the younger cousins came out onto the front porch, spotted us, and sprinted over.

"Why do they follow me everywhere?" Jenny complained.

"Because you're the queen," I said, turning to a blank page in my sketchpad and starting to draw.

"Draw me riding a giraffe!" yelled Lizzy. "With cowboy boots!"

"Draw her with a muzzle," said Jenny.

"I want a muzzle!" yelled Rory, crawling on his hands and knees over to Eric and barking in his face.

"What's a muzzle?" asked Lizzy.

"You need one," said Jenny. "You all do."

Muzzles and giraffes and queens and cowboy boots, that was right up my alley.

Much better than locker rooms and dances and chemistry labs. I drew for them until dinnertime and then went in and lost myself in McGinnis ruckus, with lots of laughs and seconds on pretzel jello.

CHAPTER 6

Monday morning, I woke up determined to make up for the dance lie, and for sixth grade. I'd be extra nice to Rick. I wasn't just using him for chemistry—I actually did like him, although I didn't want to go out with him or be his new best friend. I just needed to strike the right friendly-lab-partner note, with nothing that resembled potential girlfriendliness.

I got to chemistry before he did, which hardly ever happened. I sat down and drummed my pencil eraser on the table, trying to get my face and attitude arranged to the right degree.

"Hey Max. Greetings and salutations."

Rick pulled out a chair and stepped over the back, sitting down.

"Oh, hi Rick. How was your weekend?"

"Smashing," he said. "Fabulous, really. Yours?"

"Pretty good," I said, cautiously.

"Well that's great. Hey listen, I apologize for my odd and intrusive inquiry into the details of your social engagements last Friday. I had some sort of, ah, lapse of connectivity of gray matter. Please, be assured that it won't happen again."

This was delivered as if he were reading it off a cue card. Even the hesitation sounded rehearsed.

A cue card of my own popped up, or maybe it was a conscience card. I ignored it. I couldn't explain even if I wanted to because that would mean outing Dex, which I definitely couldn't do. So telling him was as much wrong as it was right and since both were equal, it was easier not to. Besides, he'd never know unless he went with someone else, which just didn't seem that likely.

"Now," he said, breaking into my argument with my cue card. "How did you do with last Friday's lab? Did you get it written up yet?"

He flipped open his binder and pulled out his write-up.

"Let's see if we got the same numbers."

I pulled out my own notebook and we compared. I had, of course, put a decimal point in the wrong place and messed up the whole thing. By the time we got that figured out and corrected, Ms. Patterson had closed the door and started class. Rick had let me so smoothly off the hook that I couldn't go back and fix things without making an even bigger mess. Not unless I wanted to really badly. And I didn't.

After class I found Tay down in the Commons, building a teepee of fries around a mound of ketchup.

"What's wrong?" I asked, sliding in next to her.

"Nothing," she said, pouring milk into her teepee to make a white stream through the red mound.

"Right," I said. "Nothing. Nada. That's why you're making french-fry soup, right?"

Tay shrugged.

If she didn't want to say I wasn't going to drag it out of her. She had a couple of dry fries left on her plate, so I took one. After a few more minutes of sulking she huffed away from the table, leaving a wake of bumped people and glares behind her. She dumped her trash into the can and tossed her red plastic tray toward the pile. It slid off and clattered on the floor as she disappeared around the corner.

"Hey Max, all by your lonesome?"

I caught a whiff of aftershave as Dex sat down next to me.

"Hi Dex," I said.

"Why so serious? You ought to be busy celebrating your good luck at finally getting a date with me."

He doctored his burger with ketchup and mustard.

"Something's up with Tay," I said. "She's all in a mood."

"Mmm, I bet. She must've heard about Coach Lavin."

"What about him?"

"He's not coaching this year. His wife's sick."

"Not coaching?" I asked, starting to get it. "Uh-oh."

"It gets worse. Ms. Nelson's going to coach."

"Ms. Modern Dance Nelson? Are you kidding? Does she even know the first thing about hockey?"

"Probably not," said Dex. "I wouldn't be too happy about it if I was Tay."

"I'd better go try to find her," I said, finishing my brownie.

"Go on, then. Break my heart again. Can I have your pickle?"

"Sure," I said, "if you'll dump my tray for me."

I stopped at the corner of the Commons to look back at him. Sean's boyfriend. Who ever would've thought?

I didn't find Tay until after school. She was headed across the back parking lot, her hoodie pulled up over her head.

"Tay!" I called. "Wait up a minute!"

She stopped but didn't turn around. She had her hands stuffed in her pockets, shoulders hunched against the wind. I caught up to her and we both started walking. A few dry, shriveled leaves skittled across the blacktop.

"Dexter told me about Coach Lavin," I said. "And about Nelson coaching. I'm sorry, Tay."

"I'm not playing for Nelson, that's for damn sure."

"That's kind of extreme," I said. "I mean, I know you don't like her, but maybe you can just kind of ignore her. You are her star player, after all."

"I'm not *her* star player, Max!" She whipped around

to stare at me. "I'm not *her* anything! How can you even say that?"

"Hey, hey, sorry. You're right. Not her anything. But shouldn't you talk to Coach Lavin about it? Maybe he'll have an idea what to do."

"Nah," said Tay as we came to the end of the parking lot and cut across the dead grass to the sidewalk. "He's got enough to worry about. His wife has breast cancer and it's not the first time. It's not the kind you beat. It's the other kind."

"Oh."

Cars poured out of the student lot, the bass of speakers shaking our feet as they passed.

"Have you thought about playing on the boys' team?" I asked.

"Sure, right, I'm going to play against Brett and watch his father cheer against me, if I even got to play, which you know wouldn't happen and even if it did, Feltz and Chioles and the rest of those guys would never deal with a girl on their team."

"Well that's just stupid," I said. "You're better than any of them. They should be begging you to play."

We kicked along the sidewalk, and the gray wind rattled brown leaves and bare branches overhead.

"You know, Max," said Tay. "Maybe it's actually a good thing. I've been thinking about it all afternoon. Maybe I'm kind of tired of hockey. I've been playing every year since I was what, seven? I almost like the idea of taking a year off. Anyway, I'll make a lot more money. Smell those refried beans calling me in."

She swung her backpack off her shoulders as we came up to the Taco Bell.

"Thanks for walking me over," she said. "You want a taco or something?"

"No thanks."

She went in the side entrance and I stood alone in the windy parking lot, watching the door close behind her.

Who would Tay be without hockey? I couldn't even imagine.

CHAPTER 7

The night of the dance, Tay was watching out the window of my bedroom for our dates while I sat on my bed with *People* magazine, drawing cartoon versions of movie stars.

"Omigod," she said. "They actually got a limo."

I jumped up to look. A uniformed driver with a cap opened the door, and Dexter stepped onto the sidewalk, followed by Sean. We hurried downstairs and out the front door.

"Hey, there they are!" called Sean.

"All right, check those ladies out," said Dex. "Let's go dance!"

He jumped sideways and slammed into Sean. They both looked great, laughing and moshing into each other under the streetlight. Tay looked good too, in a short hoodie over a skintight tank top and raggedy cargo pants.

I tried to tell myself that it was all about the lighting and I looked great too, but I didn't believe me. I'd bought a new top and belt and wore my favorite perfect-fit jeans, but they just made me look more like me. That was the hardest part about doing things with Tay or Sean, and now with Dexter—all three of them had a dash of hot spice in their looks. I had no spice. Not even ketchup.

"Hey, Paul!" my Dad called, coming out the door behind us.

The driver waved. I recognized him as one of Uncle Max's friends. Mom came out with the camera, and we did the obligatory pre-dance pictures. Then Paul opened the door and the boys dove into the back.

"So much for chivalry," I said to Tay as we slid in behind them.

Sean opened the little fridge and passed sodas around to everyone. I pointed to the empty pizza box on the floor.

"I guess you guys have been riding around for a while?"

"If you don't turn the volume down," said Tay as Sean put an arm around Dex, "You're gonna out your-selves to the whole school just by stepping out of the limo."

"Who cares?" asked Dex, planting a kiss on Sean.

It wasn't a big sloppy tongue kiss or anything, but it was a real one, and watching them gave me a sort of warm squishy feeling.

I looked over at Tay. She had a finger down her throat, retching.

"Come on," she said. "We'll do this date stuff with

you, but don't make us sit here and watch you climb all over each other."

Sean grinned at me. He was as happy as I'd ever seen him, and Sean is by nature a pretty happy guy. He tried to lick Dexter's ear. Dexter pulled away and swatted at him, and turned up the music.

When we pulled up in front of the gym Sean got out of the car and bowed, looking at Tay.

"My lady?" he said, all campy, holding out his arm.

Tay rolled her eyes and got out of the car. Then she did the long-blonde-hair flip, like her hair weighed about forty pounds, and minced along at his side. Dex and I followed. The vibrations of the bass poured out the gym doors.

The place was packed. The air was thick with noise and shimmied with sound and flashing lights. The four of us moved onto the dance floor, carving out a little spot for ourselves.

Tay was a great dancer. She had that ability to send different parts of her body in different directions at the same time, creating a flowing whole. She grabbed the music and wrestled with it. The music spun her, jerked her, and shook her around, push and pull, back and forth, weaving on ice.

Sean was Snoopy, nothing but joy and happy feet. Even his ears danced.

As soon as he started moving, Tay stopped having her own private conversation with the music and invited Sean in, and the two of them were gone.

They left Dexter and me behind. I tried to look

relaxed but I wasn't, and he wasn't doing much better. No conversation with the music, no takeover by the beat. We were just two kids dancing, trying to look like we were having fun.

Dex and I left the floor after a couple of tunes. He went off to mingle and I wandered in and out of the bathroom. I looked around for Tay when a slow song started. I spotted Dex dancing with a sophomore cheerleader, and Sean was up on the bleachers with a couple of drama guys. There's no place like a crowded gym for feeling alone.

Finally Tay appeared, moving through the crowd near the back doors. I waved her over.

"Heyyyy," she said, and I knew right away she'd been smoking. Then, as if she'd just read my thoughts off of a balloon over my head, she said, "I only had a couple of hits, I mean, no athletic code for Tay this year, right? So who cares?"

I did. I hated it when she got high. I folded my arms and turned away from her, looking out across the floor. The music changed, and Sean came up from behind us and pulled Tay out to dance.

"Wanna?" Dex asked at my shoulder, nodding toward the floor.

"Not really," I said.

"Me neither," said Dex. "Let's go lean on the wall."

Just the sort of thing I'd never think of on my own. Don't stand like a dummy, go lean on the wall. It was too loud to talk, so I relaxed and let my vision fuzz over. The bodies on the floor merged into one big seething, pulsing creature. And then I got a sudden whiff of something that interrupted my space-out. I blinked and looked around.

"Dex, do you smell fish?" I yelled.

"What?"

"Fish! Doesn't it smell kinda fishy in here?"

Dex sniffed.

"I don't smell anything," he said. "Want to go outside and get some air?"

The fishy smell disappeared as we moved along the wall, pinballed through the crowd by the door, and broke out into the cool night air. We found a spot on the steps and sat side by side. The wind moved through the treetops, but there was no bite to it.

"Thanks for doing this," said Dex. "Are you having fun at all?"

"Sure," I said quickly.

He looked at me sideways.

"I mean, sure I am."

He kept looking at me.

"I'm just not very good at the high-school game, that's all," I said.

"The high-school game," said Dex, shaking his head.

"What? You're great at it. A pro. Football hero

and all."

"Yeah, I bought it myself until I met Sean. I mean, I thought the game was real. But it's like I was a video game character, running around every time someone hits a button, do this do that, and I didn't even know it. Like racking up points all over, but what for? I didn't even know I wasn't running the controls."

He glanced over at me to see if I was following him. "You know?" he asked.

"Whoever's running me fell asleep or something. Or maybe their batteries ran out."

Dex laughed.

"Maxie, I think you're like Sean. You get it that it's just a game. Most of them," and he gestured at the gym, "they don't even know. They think this part is real. Like it's really crucial if we win a football game or get chosen for homecoming court or whatever. But what I can't figure out is, what about what comes next? Is that just a game, too? I mean, when is it ever real?"

"I guess it's real when you make it real," I said.

"Well, it seems real with Sean. He's the most real guy I ever met, and he's the one who makes high school seem not real. You know what I mean?"

I did.

"There was this one time when we were kids," I said. "Maybe five and six, and we were driving from Chicago with Sean's mom. We stopped at a rest stop and it was like six million degrees out, and Sean's mom locked the keys in the car. And she was so pissed, she kicked the door and kind of slammed back against the car next to us, and the car alarm goes off, scared the crap out of all of us. But then Sean started dancing."

"Dancing?"

"Yeah, dancing, like it was the best music he'd ever heard. People actually stopped and crowded around to watch him."

Dex laughed and his eyes shined up, thinking about it.

"Everyone started laughing and clapping, and then some guy helped Aunt Lisa get the keys out."

"Who else do you know who could pull off something like that?" said Dex, shaking his head.

"Nobody. That's why he's the family superstar."

"You got some good bloodlines going there," said Dex, which I thought was extra nice of him.

Suddenly, a whole wave of kids spilled out of the gym, almost running us over, and we jumped up.

"What's going on?" Dex asked a guy.

"Stink bomb in the gym," he said. "It reeks in there."

Dex and I started up the stairs. I was scanning for Sean or Tay when I locked eyes with Rick. My stomach jumped up into my throat and then did a quick drop to my feet. He was standing off to the side by the far door, leaning against the wall, staring at me. Someone passed between us and I knocked into someone else, and when I looked back again he was gone.

We pushed our way upstream through the crowd and I kept an eye out for Rick, my head spinning with what I would say to him. It came up at the last minute, didn't know I was going, favor for Sean, meant to tell you...

The smell was everywhere. Fish and something else, something thick and heavy that crawled inside my nostrils and set up camp. The music had stopped and the lights came up.

"Dex!"

I heard Sean yell and then spotted him and Tay coming through the crowd. Tay had her shirt pulled up over her nose.

"What the hell is that?" asked Dexter.

"I don't know," said Sean. "Let's get out of here."

He led the way, clearing a path through the lobby. We went down the stairs and onto the lawn as the gym emptied itself out and cars revved to life in the parking lot. Sean pulled out his cell and called Paul and we sat on the grass, back in the shadows, listening to people. I shivered a little, wishing I'd brought a jacket. I hadn't counted on sitting around outside for very long.

"I TOLD you I smelled fish," said a girl who was walking by. "Didn't I tell you an hour ago that I smelled fish?"

"Yeah baby, you told me," said her boyfriend.

"Damn straight I told you, fool," she said.

"I TOLD you I smelled fish," I said to Dexter.

"Yeah baby, you told me," he said, and turned to Sean. "She did tell me."

"Never doubt Maxie's nose," said Sean, moving a

little closer to Dex.

Watching Dexter walk around school being Mr. Football, I never could have guessed who he really was. Way more than a pretty face. No wonder Sean was crazy about him. It was nice that he'd said I was like Sean, although I was about as much like Sean as Tay was like the head cheerleader.

She knocked my elbow as she flopped back, looking up at the sky.

"What do you think that smell was?" she asked. "Besides the fish smell, I mean. That other one, it was like, I don't know, like melting gym socks. Like someone set up a campfire in the locker room and started cooking gym socks. The stinkiest most putrid ones they could find. And maybe some jock straps. Or do you think it was some kind of poison gas? Do you think we're gonna die?"

"I doubt it," said Sean. "It didn't smell chemical, more like some really bad food or something. Or yeah, gym socks."

"As long as it wasn't poison," said Tay, going on in her stoned voice. "I mean, I'm wearing my official plastic student ID doggie tag around my neck, isn't that supposed to keep me safe? Isn't that what they're for? To protect us from Columbiners and nine-eleveners? Like a magic pass to safety? Isn't that why we wear them? Look, I've got mine on."

Tay waved her ID card. Sean looked sideways at me and mimed smoking a joint. I nodded.

"It's not enough we have to wear them to school, we

even have to wear them to the freakin' dance so they can always ID us, walk right up and know our student number, boom, identified, like, what, was I dancing wrong, are you going to report me for dancing in a way that threatens the homeland, can you..."

I nudged Tay to shut her up.

"What?" she said. "I'm just asking. I mean, I have a right to ask, right? If I have to wear the doggie ID tag, then I have a right to ask. Right?"

"Right, Tay," I said. "Hey, did any of you see Rick Nash in there? I thought I saw him outside."

"Rick? No," said Sean. "Who would he come with?"

Tay should have realized I'd been busted on my technicality, but it didn't even register. She just kept staring at the sky, twirling her ID card.

The limo finally pulled up to the curb. I jumped up, rubbing my upper arms. I'd started to get really cold sitting there in the dark. The limo seats were heated, nice and cozy. Tay gave Paul her address, so whether she forgot or didn't feel like it, the plan to stay over at my house was cancelled. Whatever. Tay stoned was like no Tay at all.

We dropped her off, and then Paul stopped at my house. I got out of the car and stood alone on the sidewalk as the limo pulled away. All the times I'd looked at limos and wondered who was inside... this time it was Sean and Dex, all wrapped up in their own warm little tinted-glass world.

CHAPTER 8

The week after the dance, Rick acted so completely normal and regular that I convinced myself I hadn't seen him there at all. It had only been a split second in the middle of that noisy confusion—maybe I'd imagined it. Some residual guilt or something, which was kind of a waste because Rick didn't seem to be bothered at all.

October moved into November, football season ended, and basketball started. Tay and I got to the season-opening pep rally early so we could stake out seats on the top row of bleachers, our backs up against the wall. Kids filled in around us. Rick came in and sat alone off to our left toward the bottom. He had a circle of open space around him until Feltz and Chioles and their pals came in. Jordan nudged Lance and the whole bunch filed into the row behind Rick.

"Uh oh," said Tay, nodding in their direction. "That smells bad."

Lance leaned forward and said something in Rick's

ear. Rick stared straight ahead, but his ears changed color.

"I hope this doesn't get ugly," Tay said.

Jordan reached over and flicked one of Rick's ears. Rick turned around, and all three guys behind him pointed at each other. He faced front, both ears lit up like Rudolph's nose.

The gym was full and the boys' basketball coach started talking. Jordan reached over to the other ear— flick.

Rick turned around again and stared straight at Lance. Lance pointed at Jordan, but Rick kept looking at Lance, and his eyes narrowed down to slits. Lance said something to Jordan and they both laughed, but Rick never moved. He just laser-beamed on Lance. The same lasers I'd almost convinced myself I hadn't seen outside the dance.

"Woof, look at that!" said Tay. "It's working!"

Jordan shifted away from Lance, leaning out of the line of eyeball fire. Lance looked across the floor like he didn't notice, and Rick kept staring. A green-eyed gunshot glare, right through Lance's face. Even from ten rows up, it made me squirm.

Finally, Rick faced front. As soon as he did, Jordan and Lance looked at each other, and their shoulders went down a notch. I let my breath out.

"Wow, that was intense," said Tay. She shuddered. "Brrrr."

The coach was introducing the boys' team, and Dexter ran onto the floor.

"You're staring," said Tay out of the side of her mouth.

"I am not," I said.

"If Dex had brains half as good as his looks, he'd pick you over his current choice by a mile."

"If Dex were picking anyone like me over anyone like his current choice, it wouldn't be me and you know it."

"You're still staring," she said.

"So what? It's like watching pretty people in the movies, the ones you know you can never have."

The pep band started up, and Jordan waved hula-hands over Rick's head, but he was very careful not to touch.

"That is one stupid guy," said Tay.

She took a pen out of her pocket and threw it. It hit Jordan in the back of the neck. He spun around, and we both looked away. Nobody had seen her do it. I almost laughed out loud.

The girls' coach introduced all of her players, and then the cheerleaders went into their routine.

"How they can call that a sport," said Tay, shaking her head.

"Can you do that?" I asked as one of the cheerleaders did a flip in the air and came down into the arms of three others.

"Why would I want to?"

"Are you sure about not playing?" I asked her. "There's still a week of tryouts left."

"Positive. One hundred percent. I talked to Tamara this morning and she told me Nelson is a certified idiot on ice. You couldn't pay me to show up for that."

The cheerleaders made us all stand up and do a stupid cheer. We sat down and the principal made his stock speech about school spirit, and then he decided we'd pepped enough and he let us go.

I spotted Sean climbing down the bleachers on the other side. He looked up and waved at me, and I waved back. He'd been so wrapped up in Dexter and his drama classes at the university, I'd barely seen him since the dance.

"Alonna's having a party after the game tonight," said Tay as we stepped off the bleachers. "Wanna go?"

"Mmmm, I don't think so," I said.

"Why not?"

The crowd pushed us along through the gym doors and into the hallway.

"I just don't feel like it."

"Why are you such a snob to them?"

"Snob?" I said, stopping. "What are you talking about? I'm not a snob."

"Yes you are." She turned to face me and people had to walk around us. "Anytime I say something about Alonna or Sara or any of them, you get this look on your face. It's so obvious."

I shook my head and started walking again.

"Tay, it's not that, I like them fine. It's just...all they want to do is get high."

"Just because it gave you a headache that one time," she said. "So what, you're never going to try it again? Max, you gotta learn how to have some fun."

"Well hey Tay, I'm sorry if I'm all of a sudden not fun enough for you."

I turned off and went down the hall to my right. I walked slowly though, waiting for Tay to follow me and say that's not what she meant. When I got to the end of the hall, I turned and looked back. Tay wasn't there, but Rick came out of the boys' bathroom.

"Hey Max," he said. "What are you doing down here?"

"Nothing," I said. "I just, I don't know, I..."

"You want a ride home?" he asked. "It's getting kind of nasty outside. Sleet."

His eyes were open and friendly. Hard to believe they were the same eyes I'd seen at the rally, and maybe at the dance. If he'd really looked at me like that then, how could he look at me like this now?

"I go right by your house," he said.

I still hesitated.

"It's just a ride home," he said slowly, enunciating as if maybe I didn't quite understand the language. "Because of poor weather conditions."

"Okay," I said. "Okay, sure. I have to go up and get my jacket though."

"I'll wait. Meet me at that side door, the one by the locker room."

I ran upstairs to my locker, looking around for Tay as I went. I didn't see her anywhere, so I grabbed my stuff and ran back downstairs. The halls were pretty much cleared out. Nobody around to see me leaving with Rick Nash. I didn't like that I felt relieved about that, any more than I liked him being able to read my hesitation so easily.

"Have you started the lab report yet?" he asked, as we walked across the parking lot.

"No, but I've got all the notes with me. I'll type it up over the weekend and email it to you."

"Okay, but go easy on the font changing, okay?"

"It makes it more interesting."

"Yeah, sure, but I don't think Patterson's after interesting."

"All right, all right."

As we came up to a dark blue Explorer, he hit the remote and beeped the doors open.

"Wow," I said. "Is this yours?"

"Not yet, but it will be. My sisters got new cars for graduation. Me, I'll get the used Exploder if I manage to graduate."

"Why wouldn't you graduate?" I asked.

Rick shrugged, turning to look over his shoulder as he backed out of the lot. I clicked my seat belt.

"So how long has Sean been seeing this Dexter fellow?" Rick asked.

"Uh, just since August," I said, taken by surprise. "How'd you know?"

"I'm observant. I bet that would give some people a

shock, to find out Dexter's of the gay persuasion."

"Don't tell," I said, regretting the words before they even got out of my mouth.

The windshield wipers swooshed sleet off the glass, echoing my words in a continuous *squeak-thump*.

"I'll resist the urge," he finally said, "to spread it around school. We don't want to see little Dexter get teased."

The air blowing out of the vents no longer felt cold—now it was hot. Too hot. I might as well have sat next to Lance and flicked Rick's ears myself. No, I don't want to ride with you because you might ask me out even though I'm a gutless wonder who lied to you about going to the dance and oh by the way, would you mind protecting the football hero who actually is gay from everyone who hassles you for being gay?

He probably wished he'd left me to walk home in the sleet.

"How are your folks?" he asked. "Does your dad still make those fantastic gooey brownie things?"

"Yup."

"You've got some nice folks," he said, pulling up to the curb in front of my house. "Tell them I said hi."

"I will. And Rick, thanks for the ride. You're right,

it's really nasty out."

"My pleasure," said Rick. "Anytime. Have a good weekend."

I stood on the sidewalk and watched as he pulled out, his tires spinning a bit in the slushy mess. He really was a nice guy.

CHAPTER 9

Starting with that day of the sleet storm, November put an icy gray grip over everything. Tay and I typically had a fight once a year or so, and I kept telling myself we were getting this year's out of the way early. We'd have a snit like the one after the pep rally, and then Tay would disappear for a few days until she got over it.

This one lasted longer. She didn't call all week. She didn't show up in the Commons until the first bell. We ate lunch together but she might as well not have been there—she hardly said three words. And she didn't call me once over the weekend.

On Monday of the second week, I tried to put an end to it.

"So," I said at lunch, pedaling up-hill against the silence. "How was your weekend?"

"Work," she said, picking up her fork.

"All weekend?"

"Yup."

The Commons, as usual, buzzed with noise. A few tables away, a group of kids started up a rhythm of sputting and pounding on the table. A tall, skinny Somali guy climbed on a chair, rapping rapid-fire. I couldn't understand the words from where I sat, but they must have been good because everyone around him was laughing like crazy, high-fiving each other. He tried to step down and they pushed him back up again, slamming up the volume on the beat.

"Tay, don't be mad at me anymore."

"Who says I'm mad? I'm just tired. I've been working all the time."

"Oh. Okay."

She ate like a machine, fork to food, fork to mouth. Chew chew chew, drink milk, smash carton, done.

"Gotta go," she said. "I didn't finish my history homework yet."

If I could have thought of one single thing I'd done wrong, I would have said I was sorry just to get things back to normal, but I couldn't figure out what to apologize for. She was the one who'd said I was no fun. So we dragged through a second week, and I definitely wasn't liking Tay without hockey. It looked a lot like Tay without Tay.

By Saturday I got desperate enough for entertainment that I called Aunt Mary and offered to take her kids to any movie they wanted to see if she'd pick me up and drop us off at the mall. I was hoping for animation, but my cousins were all about the new dog movie, so I sat through ninety minutes of cuteness, broken up by three trips to the bathroom.

Sunday morning I woke up way too early and stared at the ceiling. What was I going to do all day? I tried going back to sleep and had almost made it when Mom called up the stairs.

"Max, are you awake?"

The smell of waffles wafted up to me. No way I was going to sleep with that going on.

"Breakfast is almost ready." Mom didn't think highly of sleeping past nine. "Do you want a waffle?"

"I guess so," I said.

"What?"

"I SAID, I GUESS SO!"

Pause.

"Well, come on then. Nobody's bringing you breakfast in bed, my diva."

I got up, slumped into sweats, and slouched my way downstairs. "Morning, Max," said Dad, putting down the newspaper. "Happy Sunday."

I slid into the chair across from him, scrunched down, and stared out the window at the dull gray sky. No snow yet, just brown frozen yards and ugly naked trees. The kitchen was warm though, full of coffee and waffles. Mom stood at the waffle iron, her hair matted on one side and standing up on the other.

"Who loves you?" asked Dad.

I sighed. "Not now, Dad. Okay?"

He sat there across the table from me with his patient brown eyes, his almost bald head, and his crooked smile and asked again.

"Who loves you?"

"Dad, I'm not six, okay? You can't expect me to get happy every time you play the *Who Loves You* game."

"Who loves you?"

I leaned back in my chair and closed my eyes. Table fun with Dad might be too high of a price to pay for a waffle. I opened my eyes when I heard one slide onto my plate. It sat there, fat and warm in front of me. I reached for the butter. Mom snatched the butter dish and held it over my head.

"I think your father asked you a question."

"Why are you ganging up on me?" I asked.

Dad persisted. "Who loves you?"

"You do, Dad. Now can I have the butter?"

"Who else?" he asked, while Mom continued to hold the butter over my head.

I shook my head. Sometimes it seemed like they were the kids and I had to indulge them. I sat up straight in my chair and recited.

"Mom. Dad. Grandma and Grandpa. All of the McGinnises. And Aunt Polly and Uncle Pete, even though they live in Arizona and I haven't seen them in almost two years."

Mom gave me the butter dish. They exchanged a glance, and Dad shrugged.

I slathered butter on my waffle and watched it melt and fill up the holes. How was I ever going to grow up and go live in the world? My parents were annoying, but they didn't get randomly mad at me for weeks at a time. They fed me waffles no matter what. Mom set a glass of milk in front of me, just as I wished I had one.

"What are your plans for tonight?" she asked.

I shrugged, taking another big bite. The little pockets held all the warmth and sweetness of the butter and syrup.

"What's Tay up to?" asked Dad.

"Living in the land of Taco Bell. That's all she does now."

"It's such a shame about her quitting hockey," said Mom. "It always seemed to me like that was the one thing keeping her on track. That and you, of course."

Not anymore.

"Is she doing all right?" asked Dad.

"I guess."

"And how about Rod Nash?" asked Mom. "How's he getting along?"

"It's Rick, Mom. He's fine. Oh, I forgot—he said hi. He gave me a ride home that day it was sleeting."

"He was always such an odd little duck," said Mom.

"Well, he's a big duck now. Is there any more waffle batter?"

"Nope, that was the last of it. Do you want a bowl of cereal?"

I shook my head and ran my finger around the edge of the plate to catch the leftover syrup.

"What time are we going out to the Grands' today?"

"We're not going this week. I've got to finish this brief."

You'd think she'd slapped me, the way the tears came

gushing up into my eyes. I ducked my head.

"Maxie, honey, what's wrong?"

"It's just dumb," I said, looking at my plate. "Tay's mad at me and I don't know why."

"Have you asked her?" asked Dad.

"It's Tay. She says, oh, I'm not mad." I sniffed hard, making myself quit crying. "But she is."

"Oh hon," Mom put her hand on my shoulder. "You make me so glad I'm not sixteen. Why don't you call Sean and ask him to take you out to the Grands'? That'll do you some good."

"In case you haven't noticed, Sean doesn't go out there anymore. He's too busy with Dex-ter." I said it with a snotty little two-syllable stomp on Dexter's name, like I was six years old.

"How about a couple of games of Parcheesi with the old man, then? Or we could go out there, just the two of us."

"Or you could do a little surfing on schools and give that some thought," said Mom. "Figure out which ones you want to visit and make a list so we can plan our trips."

I sucked in a big breath, dragging in all the air in the kitchen and some from the living room too, then heaved it out.

"Come on," said Mom, rubbing my shoulders. "C'mon, champ. You can sit around and mope all day, or you can get in there and do something. What do you say?"

"Fine. I'll surf. Big fun."

I helped clean up the dishes and went back to my room with every intention of thinking about college. But I got distracted by a book Uncle Max had given me a few years ago about sketching animals. I'd paged through it at the time but never tried any of the exercises in it.

I grabbed a sketchbook and pencil, and a couple of hours slipped by. When I drifted downstairs to graze around in the refrigerator, Mom was in her office with the door shut, and Dad was reading in the living room. I kind of hoped he'd offer again to go out to the Grands', but I didn't want to ask. He was happy where he was. He'd only offered because he felt sorry for me. That made two of us.

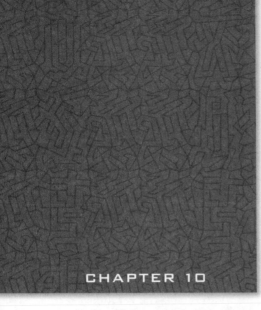

CHAPTER 10

Monday morning, Tay came sailing across the Commons, her old Converse sneakers sliding on the linoleum floor.

"Guess what?" she said, like the past two weeks hadn't happened. "Guess what guess what guess what?"

"Coach Lavin's coming back?" I asked.

"No no no. Better even. Brett's father had a guilt attack and you'll never guess what he gave me."

"A car?"

"Okay, not that good. But almost. A snowboard!"

"Oh, hey, you've been wanting to try that."

"Yeah, I love it when those daddy guilties kick in. Board, boots, helmet, wrist guards. The works. Now all I need is some snow. Wanna go with me? You could rent one."

"I guess. If you think I'm fun enough."

"Oh Maxie. Are you still mad about that? That's been weeks ago. Come on, lighten up!"

That was Tay. Storm gone, skies blue, forget about

the puddles. And I was so relieved to have her back, I was perfectly happy to let it go.

That week was a short one because of Thanksgiving. The sky stayed stingy and gray, not giving us sun or snow—just a biting breeze that shoved the windchill down below zero. Tay checked the long-term weather forecasts and tracked every storm that started on the west coast.

"When does it usually start snowing?" she asked me. "Doesn't it start in November? Don't you think we should have some by now?"

"No, we don't usually get it to stick until December. Remember the whole 'Are we going to have a white Christmas' question? Hey, are you coming on Thanksgiving? It should be good—Sean's bringing Dexter to meet the family."

"Hate to miss a scene like that, but I'm working," she said, standing up and putting her bookbag over her shoulder.

"On Thanksgiving? Who goes to Taco Bell on Thanksgiving?"

"My mom, remember?"

"Oh right," I said. That was how Tay started coming out to the Grands' for dinner. In eighth grade, when my mom asked about her Thanksgiving plans, Tay said she and her mom were going to McDonald's. From that point on, they had a standing invitation, although Tay's mom never came. "You know my grandpa's going to be disappointed."

"Thanks, but tell him I get double pay. He'll understand that, value of a dollar and all. If it ever snows, I'm going to need money for lift tickets."

"Okay, I'll tell him, but he's not going to like it. He'll tell you to come and play in the snow at their house."

When I got to chemistry fourth period, someone had drawn a huge turkey with a Santa cap on the white board in front.

"Fa la la, now we start the holiday season," said Rick, jerking his head toward it. "I can hardly wait. How about you?"

"Not so bad," I said. "All my cousins come out to my grandparents' farm. Lots of food, lots of noise. My head rings for about three weeks after. About the time I get recovered, we do it all over again at Christmas."

"Noise. Huh. There's a concept. We don't have a lot of that at my house. Although we'll have more tomorrow, what with the infants phenomenon coming home tonight."

"The what?"

"You remember my sisters, don't you?"

I did, vaguely. The twins had been sleek and glossy cheerleaders when we were kids. Roddy was the scraggly mutt in a family of purebreds.

"Sure, but what did you call them?"

"Infants phenomenon. It's from *Nicholas Nickleby*, you know, Dickens? Did you read it?"

"Isn't that about a million pages long with small print?"

"Yeah, but it's funny. Anyway, that's what this guy in the book calls his daughter and it fits the twin unit perfectly. They're home from France so we're all very joyous in the Nash household. My mother might even get out of bed for a day or two."

"Oh," I said, as Ms. Patterson came in and opened her book on the table up front. "That sounds, ah, good?"

"Heavy emphasis on *sounds*," said Rick. "I'll be spending most of the weekend in my room. With any luck, Patterson will dish out some kind of fun with chemistry I can work on."

She didn't. She sprung us without a single shred of homework.

"No luck for you," I said to Rick as we picked up our books.

"Typical. I'll have to find other ways to entertain myself. Hey, enjoy your functional family with their happy noise."

We walked out the back door of the classroom together, into the swarm of lunchtime locker-banging.

"Hey Roddy!" someone called in a falsetto voice off to our left. Rick stiffened beside me. "Rodddeeee, come and suck my rod, Roddeeeee!"

His face went purple-red under the acne.

"Later Max," he said, making a sharp right.

I backed up against the wall and watched him go, his head bobbing above the rest of the crowd until he turned the corner. Why couldn't everyone just leave him alone?

On the way out to the Grands' the next day, I thought about what Rick said—functional family. I mean, we had our stuff. Several divorces, single mom giving her kid to gay uncles to raise, my youngest uncle Jack who'd become a father in ninth grade, and Aunt Mary's little drunk driving problem. The aunts and uncles all made jokes about our dysfunctional family but when you came right down to it, we actually did function pretty well. Kids got taken care of, holidays got celebrated, birthdays got sang for. Whatever went on at the Nash house, it was hard to imagine when I was cozied up at the Grands'.

Thanksgiving unfolded the same as always—food, noise, and football. I was on the edge of the couch, though, waiting for Sean and Dexter to arrive. The McGinnis family had already absorbed all kinds of in-laws and friends and strays, so I didn't think anything would go too wrong. But it'd be fun to watch Dexter navigate the waters. I hoped Sean had coached him on good humor and rolling with the verbal punches.

They arrived in the middle of a close football game.

"Hey Gramps," said Sean, "I'd like you to meet Dexter Jones."

"I don't care who the hell he is, I'm watching the game."

A look of pure panic ran across Dexter's face, but Sean rolled his eyes and grabbed the remote from the arm of Grandpa's chair. He clicked off the TV.

"Is that any way to treat a guest?" he asked. "That's not how I was raised."

Grandpa groaned up out of his recliner.

"We won't go into how you were raised," he said. Then he turned to Dexter and shook his hand. "It's a pleasure to meet you, young man. Welcome to our home. I'm going to assume the very best about you despite the company you keep. Sean, give me back that remote before I clock you one."

Dexter gave his best winning smile and grabbed the remote from Sean.

"Here you go, sir," he said. "Sorry about the interruption."

Grandpa spent all afternoon asking the rest of us, from Sean down to one-year-old Mikey, who couldn't even talk, why we couldn't be as decent and respectful as young Mr. Jones.

I sidled next to Uncle Greg as we gathered in the kitchen for the prayer.

"So?" I whispered. "What do you think?"

"He makes Sean study," said Greg. "So I think he can stay around."

"Sean just tells you that so you'll think he's a good influence."

"I know. It works."

After our typical twenty-minute circle of soppy gratitude prayers we charged the serving table and loaded up. I used my elbows to clear a path for Dexter, since Sean had left him to figure it out on his own.

"Get in here," I said, "or there won't be anything left but a few bones."

"Thanks," said Dexter, moving in behind me. "How am I doing?" he whispered in my ear.

"Terrific. Keep it up with the sirring and ma'aming and you're in. Although I'm not sure why you'd want to be."

"You kidding?" he asked. "Everyone's a comedian here, it's great. If sir is what it takes, sir is what they'll get. Grab me that drumstick, would you?"

CHAPTER 11

After Thanksgiving we were, as Rick had pointed out, on the fast track toward Christmas vacation. Tay became completely obsessed with meteorology, giving me the daily weather report.

One morning in the Commons, she said, "What if it doesn't snow all winter?"

"It'll snow, Tay. It's still early December."

"If I have to wait till after Christmas I'll slit both wrists. I'm already about to slit one. Do you know there's no snow in the ten-day forecast? Not a flake? Nothing better than a twenty-percent chance of precipitation?"

We headed upstairs and were weaving through the crowd to our lockers when we heard a loud pop. Everyone stopped and kind of crouched, like we thought someone was going to whip out an AK-47.

Jordan Feltz backed up from his locker, shaking his right hand.

"Goddamn it!" he yelled. "What the fuck was that?

Look at my hand!"

He held it out, and we crowded around with others to see. He had a dark purplish stain on his finger and thumb.

"I just grabbed the dial on my locker, and wham," he said. "What is this shit on my hand, anyway?"

"Dude, you better go wash it off," said one of the hockey guys from behind me. "Maybe it's going to eat away your skin or something. Or maybe it's gunpowder."

"You think?" Jordan sniffed it. "Doesn't smell like anything," he said, and he headed off to the boys' bathroom, shaking his hand.

Tay and I looked at each other and shrugged. If anyone was going to get a thumb eaten away, Feltz seemed like a good choice.

Fourth period, I'd barely gotten started on the chemistry quiz when something snapped loudly behind Rick and me, like a mousetrap going off. Everyone jumped and looked around, trying to figure out where it came from.

"Keep working, please," said Ms. Patterson.

Like anyone could. We all bent over our papers and pretended to work while Patterson walked over to the back corner and bent down behind a lab table. Just then, something else banged up toward the front. A girl at the front table gave a little shriek, and *mutter mutter mutter* moved through the room.

"Continue working, please," said Ms. Patterson, the

screws tightening in her voice.

She went back to her desk and got a piece of paper and a pair of tweezers. She picked something up off the floor in the front corner and put it on the paper.

We bent over our quizzes. I felt like a prairie dog on alert, popping my head up every few seconds to look for the next bang.

I finally settled down enough to scribble some answers, but I was still the last one to turn in my paper to Ms. Patterson. By the time I got back to my seat, she was pacing the front of the room.

"Bangs and pops, all over school this morning," she said. "Got you on edge?"

Everyone nodded.

"How many?" she asked. "Hold up fingers for how many you've personally witnessed."

Feltz's locker, plus two in here. I held up three fingers. Everyone in the room, obviously, had at least two. One girl had both hands up, six fingers. Rick had three.

"Who knows what's causing it?" she asked.

Silence. No hands.

"I'll give you the clues," said Ms. Patterson. "Capsule fragments. Here, I'll pass them around," she added, and she passed around the piece of paper she'd used to scoop up whatever was on the floor.

"Drug manufacturers put medication in these—

it's easy enough to empty them out and put something else in. So what was in them? Take a look on the floor here." She pointed to the spot in the front of the room. "Or back behind that lab table. Tell me what you see."

I moved to the one in back. I didn't see anything, but I didn't know what I was looking for.

"Purple," said Tom Gilmore. He was on his hands and knees behind the lab table, eyeballing the spot so closely the rest of us couldn't see around his head. "Purple residue."

"Good, Tom. What's that mean? Do you know?"

"If I know," said Tom, standing up, "does that mean you're going to think I did it?"

Everyone stopped looking at the floor and looked back and forth between Patterson and Tom.

"You can all take your seats," she said, and we did. "A number of you in here—and in my second period class—are perfectly capable of learning about this particular reaction. Understanding the significance of purple residue does not equal a confession."

"Iodine," said Tom.

I knew he wouldn't be able to resist saying it. Besides, no one in the world was going to think Tom Gilmore had done anything like this.

"Right," said Patterson. "Iodine."

Then she launched into a long lecture about the hazards of playing around with chemicals. Safety glasses blah blah quantities blah blah impure blah clean equipment blah hazardous blah blah blah.

When we were staggering under the weight of it all,

she stopped and looked around the room, one person at a time, making eye contact.

"I like pranks," said Patterson. "I especially like smart pranks. But times are not what they used to be and every person in this room knows what I mean. So listen up and listen hard. I never—"

Pause. We all sat very still.

"Never—"

Some maverick little laugh twitched inside of me. It was all so dramatic.

"Never, under any circumstances, want to see or hear about or have any knowledge of or reason to worry about any student in this class playing any prank with chemicals in this school or anywhere else. You think you're funny, you think you're smart, maybe you're both. But don't do it. Because I'll tell you where this will go. No labs, that's where. Lectures and textbooks only, and a lousy education for all of you. Okay, and probably unemployment for me. Seriously, though, that's where this is heading. So knock it off."

She scanned, face by face. I twitched when she looked at me, even though I couldn't figure out how to explode iodine if you held a gun to my head. She kept us dead quiet until the bell rang and broke her hold, and everyone started to move and talk again.

I followed Rick out of the room, right on his heels, and grabbed him by the arm.

"So who do you think is doing the iodine tricks?"

"I don't know," he said. "Whoever it is, they'd better be careful. Patterson's no fool."

"I know, the way she looked at me I wanted to tell her everything I know, and I don't even know anything."

"You know lots," he said. "But not anything Patterson's worried about."

"Like chemistry, you mean?"

"Ha. It'd help if you read the book sometimes instead of making me do all the work."

"I work!"

He smirked and shook his head, and we went our separate ways.

CHAPTER 12

We still didn't have any good snow by Christmas break, but they'd been making it out on the slopes, so Tay and I went for a lesson. The teacher was a short thin guy named Sam, and he had the prettiest face you ever saw, smooth-cheeked and big-eyed. He tried to cover it up with a tiny bit of beard scruf—which was the only way you could tell he was older than twelve—and seven face piercings. Even though there were six of us in the class, he spent about fifty-two minutes of the hour with Tay. Every now and then, he threw a minute at the rest of us.

After the lesson he invited Tay to go on a couple of runs with him and his friends, who were definitely older than twelve. More like twenty. I spent the rest of my day trying to exit the chairlift without falling in the path of the next fifty people getting off, and watching Tay's back as she zipped off down the hill, spraying fake snow on every turn.

The phone woke me the next morning. I kept

thinking Mom or Dad should get it but then realized they must be gone to work. I rolled over and everything hurt. Every muscle. I picked up and made a little mewling sound into the phone.

"Maxie, is that you? Have you looked outside? We got that storm, it totally dumped all night long. I can come by and get you in twenty minutes."

I rolled my eyes over to look at the clock. Nine-fifteen.

"Tay, I can't even move. You go ahead."

"Can't move? Why not?"

"I don't know, maybe it was spending all of yesterday bouncing down the hill on my butt."

"You didn't do that bad, Maxie. Come on, you'll do better today. Plus all this fresh powder, it won't even hurt to fall."

"Won't hurt me, 'cause I'm not going."

After a long pause, Tay said, "Well, okay. I'm leaving pretty soon, so if you get up and decide..."

"Thanks, but I don't think so. Have fun."

I hung up and lay back with a groan. Eventually, I got up and staggered over to the window. Sparkling white covered everything. Lots of it. All waiting for me to shovel. Even if I'd wanted to, I couldn't have gone with Tay until the walk was cleared. I put on sweats and limped downstairs. By the time I felt motivated enough to layer on warm clothes, the temperature had climbed up to ten degrees.

Outside, the sun bounced off every snowflake. It was a fluffy snow, dry and light, but there was an awful lot of it. The sidewalk out front was all tromped down by everyone walking by, which would make it that much harder to shovel. I cleared the snow off the porch and started working on the walk. A car horn honked and I looked up.

Rick's Explorer pulled up next to the snowbank on the other side of the street.

"Hey, don't you believe in snowblowers?" he called.

I dropped the shovel and waded down the walk. I climbed over all the hunks and icy chunks thrown up by the plow, and out into the street.

"I do," I said. "But my parents don't."

The heater blew warm air out his open window. I moved closer to it.

"Are you kidding?" he asked. "You really have to shovel this all by yourself?"

"This isn't half of it," I said. "Don't forget the driveway in back, and the back walk. I'll be out here all day. I suppose you already did yours."

"Surely you jest," he said. "A Nash, stoop to manual labor? My mother hires some kid with a snowblower. I never touch the stuff."

"Then you should help me with mine. My parents say shoveling snow gives you moral fiber."

Rick laughed out loud.

"I guess that's what good parenting looks like, huh? Moral fiber. I like that."

"I've got an extra shovel."

Rick tilted his head and looked at me for a long moment. His eyes were clear green and friendly, like pieces of glass washed up on shore and smoothed out by the waves.

"Why not," he said. "How hard can it be?"

I hesitated. If he helped me shovel, then I'd owe him.

"You don't have to help. I was just whining. It's not that bad."

"No, no, I want to. I want to give this moral fiber thing a shot."

He got out and shut the door.

"At least let me get you a hat and some mittens," I said. "And quit when you get sick of it, okay?"

"You just don't want me to get more moral fiber than you. You're trying to keep a corner on the market."

He could be funny sometimes. I went to the garage and got him a hat and mittens and a scarf and brought back the other snow shovel. When I came around front, he'd started on the walk.

"Here," he said, handing me the shovel he'd been using. "Give me that one."

"No, it's okay."

"No, it's not," he said. "I'm new at this. The more advanced tool should go to the one who knows how to use it."

So I took back the ergonomically correct shovel that Dad had given me for my fourteenth birthday, and he took the straight-handled one.

We both dug in. On the wide part of the walk, we played snowplow and shoveled in tandem. Then we marked off other parts and raced to see who could clear first. The snow glittered in the sunshine and rainbow-shimmered when we threw it in the air. We cleared the walk, and then I started in on the next-door-neighbor's walk.

"What are you doing?" asked Rick.

"We always do Mrs. Lewis's walk."

"Wait a minute." He leaned on his shovel. "You have to do your own walk AND the neighbor's walk?"

"That's right," I said. "Community cooperation."

"Why not get a snowblower, then? You could do the whole neighborhood."

I stuck my shovel in the snow and ticked off each point of my parents' snow-shoveling rationale.

"Snowblowers contribute to global warming, plus they stink. There's value in hard work. The beauty of interacting directly with nature. Exercise and fitness. General character development. An ergonomically correct shovel doesn't interfere with the moral-fiber building, but you can't use anything with a motor, not for raking leaves either. There's fuel conservation to think about, of course, and the cost of gas. Oh, and don't forget about noise pollution. I think that about covers it."

"Huh," he said. "I had no idea there was so much to this whole snow-shoveling thing. Well, let's get on it."

We went to work on Mrs. Lewis's walk, then trudged around back. We did the walk back there and moved on to the main event, the back driveway. That hadn't been messed up yet; my parents both took the bus to work. By the time we dug through that, I had the tingling glow you get from being warm deep inside. It spilled into my muscles and chased away the tiredness.

We put the shovels in the garage and admired our work. The driveway was beautiful. We'd thrown the snow up to make high banks and scraped all the way down to pavement.

"Remember snow art?" asked Rick.

"That's been a long time ago," I said.

"Yeah, but you were good at it."

"Maybe I still am."

I ran clunky-clumsy in boots across the driveway and climbed the bank we'd just made. Little chunks of snow rolled down onto the cleared cement behind me. I got up on the highest spot I could find and turned to face Rick. I looked over my shoulder at the smooth whiteness. I spread my arms, lifted my face to the deep blue sky, and dropped straight back.

Whoosh. I landed in the softness, flakes settling on my face. They itched, but I lay still and let them melt on my skin. I opened my eyes to see Rick climbing the bank. When he got to the top, his shadow fell over me and blocked the sun from my eyes. He turned his back and stood for a long moment, arms outstretched like Jesus on the cross, and then slowly, slowly tipped back. Whoosh. He landed next to me.

We lay there side by side in silence. My breath huffed in and out, and my pulse thudded faintly in my ears. The snow held me close on all sides.

When the cold began to seep in through my clothes, I got up carefully, stepping away so I didn't ruin the print. Rick and I made more snow art, still and action poses, and then we created the shape of an elephant and a giraffe, sculpting and etching and drawing up the back yard. The cold air froze our faces so our words and our laughs came out half-speed in steamy balloons. Something about that, and the puffy jackets and the big boots clomping—it all made me feel like fifth-grade Maxie.

Rick did a dramatic swan dive and landed flat. As he got up, I threw snow at him. He threw some back, an arc of dazzle in front of my eyes. The snow was too dry to pack, but we threw armfuls back and forth, on our knees, laughing like crazy, snow sticking on eyebrows and lashes and melting on our warm red cheeks. I charged Rick and knocked him over, filling my mittens with snow and trying to pack it down his neck. He bucked around underneath me, finally knocking me off and jumping back, rolling up to his knees.

"Whoa!" he said. "Whoa, girl!"

I stopped, panting. This was the most fun I'd had in forever. Way more fun than snowboarding.

"I gotta go," he said, standing.

"Wait, don't go. I made you shovel our driveway and then I threw snow down your neck. The least I can do is make you some hot chocolate or something."

"Nope. Gotta go. The pleasure's been all mine. Here's your hat, and mittens, and scarf. Thanks for the fun and games," he said. "Oh, and the moral fiber. See you in school."

He waded through the side yard around the house and was gone before I could even pull another thought together. I stayed there on my knees in the snow, looking at the tromped-up messed-up printed-up yard. A bit of melting snow trickled down my back. I looked at our first two snow shapes, the most perfect ones we made. They were side by side. His long arm stretched toward me and his mitten-hand almost touched my shoulder.

I liked how his body print looked. You couldn't see the acne or the flickable ears or the scary slitted eyes. It was big and tall and long and friendly. Just like a stretched-out Roddy. Why couldn't he have grown up to be cool and good-looking? Wasn't there a guy somewhere who was cute and fun and not gay who would help me shovel and then play in the snow?

I flopped back and closed my eyes against the bright sun. I let the snow hold me until the cold crept in through the layers and I started to shiver. Then I got up and went inside.

CHAPTER 13

For a minute or two, it looked like Sean wasn't going to show up for Christmas dinner. In my family, that was like ignoring an invitation from the president or the Pope. Christmas Eve you could go to your other grandparents' or whatever, but dinner on the twenty-fifth at three o'clock in the afternoon was written in stone. Exceptions only if you were in the hospital or out of the country.

By dinnertime, everyone had ripped through their presents and cleaned up most of the mess. We bagged the wrapping paper and stacked our goods along the wall, and set up the long table for the cousins in the middle of the family room. Just as we were sitting down to eat, Sean slipped in through the back door. He looked terrible.

"What's up?" I whispered to him, scooting over to make room on the bench.

"After dinner," he said.

He went into the kitchen to say hi to the Grands and

fill his plate, then came out and sat next to me. As soon as we got done clearing the table, we dodged the crowd and shut ourselves up in the little den downstairs.

"What the heck is wrong?" I asked. "Grandma just about flipped when the Unks showed up without you."

Sean spun the desk chair around and sat on it backwards. I sat on the rocking chair across from him.

"Am I a racist, Maxie?" he asked.

I looked at him hard to see if he was kidding. He wasn't.

"Not that I've noticed. Why do you ask?"

"Dex and I had a pretty bad fight yesterday."

"And he called you a racist?"

"Practically. Max, I don't even know what happened. One minute we're talking about how his dad doesn't understand him, and suddenly he's yelling at me about my 'white privilege,' whatever that is, because being the class queer since kindergarten hasn't felt all that privileged to me."

"Wow," I said, shaking my head. "I thought things were perfect between you guys. Is this your first fight?"

"Yup. Really, I think he's freaking out now because his dad knows. Last week he asked Dex point blank what the nature of our relationship was, and Dex told him."

"How'd he take it?"

There was a thud at the bottom of the stairs that made us both jump, followed by a banging on the door and a high-pitched voice. "Who's in there?"

"Who wants to know?" I asked.

"Me, Lizzy. Grandma says I have to take a time-out."

"Well, go do it in the TV room. Sean and I are in here."

"Grandma said to take a time-out in there," she insisted.

"Tell her we wouldn't let you in here."

She didn't answer, but we could hear her stuffy nose breathing just on the other side of the door. Sean got up and opened it, and she almost fell in.

"What are you doing?" he asked.

"Listening."

Sean turned Lizzy upside down and carried her out by the ankles.

"I'm bigger than Grandma," he said. "And I'm telling you that you have to take your time-out in the TV room."

He closed the door.

"I'll watch TV!" she yelled.

"Go ahead," said Sean. "I won't tell on you."

He came back in and shut the door behind him.

"Where was I?" he asked.

"Dexter's dad. How'd he take it?"

"Not good. Not good at all. He thinks Dex is making a bad decision, like he'd picked the wrong school or something."

"So his dad doesn't get it about being gay, huh?"

"Nope."

"What made Dex say the white privilege thing? Did you say something stupid?"

"No, he just started yelling at me because I hadn't told him about Donovan."

"Our Donovan?"

"Yeah. I mean, the kid's only seven, I didn't even think about it. Besides, who knew he'd be here for Thanksgiving? I can't keep track of which holiday which kids are where."

"Wait, I don't get it. What did he want you to tell him?"

"That the color barrier had been broken. Turns out he was really nervous about coming into all-white McGinnis country. How was I supposed to know, it's not like he told me. I mean, could you tell he was nervous?"

"Not really," I said. "He did ask me how he was doing but not in a super-nervous way, just in a normal way."

"He was all, 'You should have known that would matter to me' and I was trying to tell him that Mary and Paul split up like five years ago, but when I said we don't even think of Donny as black because he's just ours, Dex really went ballistic. He said if I ever tried to say I was color-blind then we were done."

"Oh, wait!" I said. "I know about this. Mom went off on a thing last week about a senator who said he was color-blind. She said only white people get that luxury."

"Oh." Sean chewed on that for a minute. "So that's white privilege?"

"Wait, let me think what she said." I closed my eyes and put myself back at the kitchen table with my mom staring into my eyes and trying to make me think like she does. "She said that white people say, 'Oh, I'm color-blind,' but it's a racist culture and if you're blind you can't see it so you keep being part of it. I asked her if everyone is still racist, like every-everyone, even her, and she said of course she is but she's anti-racist too, and that takes work, and anyone who says they're color-blind isn't doing the work."

"Shit," said Sean, staring out the window at the spread of snow. "I thought color wasn't supposed to matter."

I hadn't thought about Donny while Mom was talking, but I did now. We didn't think of him as black, but he was, and probably he didn't forget it.

"So Dex's dad doesn't get it about being gay and you don't get it about being black," I said. "And you got all defensive."

"I didn't get defensive!"

He laughed at the look on my face, and then said, "Okay, maybe. Kind of. It just happened so fast, and besides, his mom's white, so I guess, I don't know. I guess I didn't think this had to be an issue."

"Sounds like it is for him."

Sean sighed. "He cut me off in the middle of trying to explain, he was out the door while I was still talking, and now he won't pick up when I call. Do you think he'll try to straighten up?"

"I don't know, can he? I mean, can someone just decide to do that?"

"Maybe some people can, if they're bi, but I really

don't think he is. He'd just make himself miserable try-ing."

"Plus he could make you miserable trying," I said.

"I'm already miserable. I'm crazy about him. I have to at least get this racist thing figured out enough so I don't make it worse, but I don't know what to do. I mean, how do I quit having white privilege?"

"I don't know, Sean," I said, shaking my head. "I think you should, you know, try to listen to him. Not so you can argue back that he's wrong—really try to get what he's saying. Or you could ask my mom about it, she—"

Feet thumped on the stairs again, and a little fist pounded on the door.

"Who's in the den?"

"Who wants to know?"

"Me. Josh. Hey, we're starting. You guys are play-ing, right?"

"Busy place," muttered Sean. "You ready to go? I could drive you home."

"Don't you want to spend a little time with Grand-ma and Grandpa first?" I asked.

"Don't guilt me, Maxie. I'll come by and see the Grands later this week. I just can't right now, you know? I gotta talk to Dex. You coming?"

I wanted to go with him. I wanted to tell him about Tay disappearing into Snowboard Land and about shov-eling snow with Rick and all the mixed-up feelings I was having.

As he twitched at the doorway I knew the conversa-

tion wouldn't happen,
even if we spent the
whole day together.
Sean had many talents,
but emotional multitask-
ing wasn't one of them.

"Nah, I'll stay," I
said. "I promised the kids a round of Twister. Let me
know what happens though, okay?"

"Okay." Sean opened the door. "Bye buddy," he
said to Josh, who was still standing there.

"Where are you going?"

"Business," said Sean, taking the stairs two at a time.

"You're playing, aren't you?" Josh asked me.

"Yeah, I'm playing."

I followed Josh upstairs to the living room and
watched out the front window as Sean's MG pulled out.

"Is he okay?" asked Uncle Max, coming up and putting an arm around me.

"I think so," I said. "He's just busy, you know, having a life."

"Maxie!" yelled Josh from the living room. "Are you
playing or not?"

"Your life is calling you," Max said, turning me
around and giving me a little shove toward the Twister
game. "Go on, you don't want to miss out."

CHAPTER 14

I tried calling Sean over the next few days, but I kept
getting his voice mail. I finally reached him on New
Year's Eve morning.

"Hey Sean, are you guys going to be there tonight?"

"Where?"

"Party? Your place? Where'd you think?"

"Oh, that. Actually, no. We're still kinda bumpy,
so we decided to go to a party on campus. Just people I
know from class, so we can stay surface and have fun."

"Oh."

That shot down my whole idea about New Year's. I
definitely wasn't going to the Unks if it was going to be
all old people.

"Thanks for the advice though." Sean kept talking.
"About listening to him. I've been trying."

"How's it going?" I asked. If Sean's love life was going to be my entertainment for the day, I might as well
find out the details.

"Hard. He's been so freaked about his dad, he's not

exactly rational."

"What about you? Are you rational?"

"I'm always rational," said Sean.

"Ha. What's up with his dad? Is it getting worse?"

"Last night his dad said, 'Fine, I can't stop you, but I hope you don't wreck your whole life before you come to your senses.' Which is better than yelling at him and calling him an idiot, but still not good."

"So if Dex is talking to you, then things must be better? Between you and him?"

"Better than it was. I googled white privilege and found a couple of good websites where I could ask some questions, so at least I'm not saying stupid stuff. But it's still hard, you know? He's touchy, and not in a good way. Hey, what are you and Tay doing tonight?"

"Tay's been hanging with snowboarder stoners. She's going to some big party with them."

"And you?"

"I don't know. I'm not up for the snowboard crowd."

"Oh." I could almost hear Sean rummaging around in his head for the right thing to say. "Listen, I'd invite you along with me and Dex only, you know, we're still kinda hashing stuff out and—"

"Forget it, Sean. Don't worry, I'm fine."

I said the same thing later to my parents as they got ready for Uncle Max's party. They didn't much believe me—Dad made sad eyes at me as they went out the door—but they went and left me home alone anyway.

I cranked up the heat and settled onto the couch

with a pint of Ben and Jerry's Chunky Monkey. I surfed all evening, mostly flicking between Times Square and *It's a Wonderful Life*. When the phone rang I figured it'd be Tay.

"Hello?" I said.

"Hi, um, Maxie?"

"Yeah, this is Maxie. Who's this?"

"Rick. Rick Nash. I just... I didn't think you'd be home. I just wanted to, you know, say Happy New Year."

"Oh. Well. Happy New Year to you, too."

"And I wanted to say I had fun. Shoveling snow with you. I..." He stopped. I waited for him to go on, but the silence stretched out bigger and longer. Then we both started to talk at once.

"Well, I just..."

"You're right," I said. "I mean, me too. I haven't had that much fun in the snow in a long time. Like forever."

"Remember the time we went sledding at that park by the river? It reminded me of that."

"Yeah," I said. "That was fun."

"We used to have some good times when we were little, huh?"

I glanced over at the TV. Girls in bikinis rocked out at a New Year's beach party.

"So," said Rick. "On your way out tonight?"

"No, I decided to just stay home. How about you?"

"Well, you know, I had too many invitations to choose from and I didn't want to pick one over another.

So in the interest of equal treatment of my many friends and admirers, I'm enjoying a peaceful evening of solitude."

"That's generous of you," I said. "Peaceful evening of solitude. Yeah, that's what I'm doing too."

"Evaluating the past year, planning your moves for next one?" he asked.

"Right. All that."

"Do you make New Year's resolutions?"

"Not really. I used to, but they never lasted more than a week. What about you?"

"Mine always last," he said. "That's why I'm so careful about making them."

"Are you making any this year?"

"Signs point to yes. Well look, I don't want to bother you or anything. I just wanted to give you my New Year's salutations so I looked your folks up in the book. Do you have a cell number?"

The next thing I knew, I was giving Rick Nash my cell number. He gave me his too, but I didn't write it down.

"Well, see you in school on Monday," he said.

We Happy New Yeared each other again and hung up.

Next morning my parents rustled around downstairs, muttering and laughing and banging things in the kitchen. They'd probably had a good time at the party. I checked my cell for a report of Tay's good time. No messages.

I reached under my bed for my sketchpad and started doodling around the edges. Before we were old enough to go out, Sean and I were always at the Grands' on New Year's. They hosted the grandkids while the parents went to parties. Sean and I were the oldest, so we were in charge. I looked forward to it for months, especially the part when everyone fell asleep and we stayed awake all night, talking and watching movies and finishing off the pizza and whatever desserts we could find lying around. Things were better back then. Simpler.

I sketched our little-kid selves.

Sean when he was chubby, Roddy with his huge ears. Tay rolling into seventh grade on blades. I looked the same when I was a kid, just shorter. I hadn't known Dexter before high school, but he was easy enough to imagine. He was probably the best kickball player in the class.

My cell phone jingled out its tune and I flipped it open.

"Knock knock," a deep voice said.

"Who's there?" I answered, grinning down at my picture of Roddy.

"New Year's."

"New Year's who?"

"Knew yer cell number so I thought I'd call. Bye now."

It felt good to laugh at a dumb knock-knock joke and not roll my eyes or look around to see who else was laughing. Just like it had felt good to play with Rick in the snow. What was wrong with old-fashioned playing?

Everything had changed in middle school, and now it was changing again. I didn't even meet Tay until we were old enough to officially quit playing, but sometimes she used to explode with happiness, like the time a tiny blue butterfly landed on her shoulder at recess and she spent the rest of the day saying she'd been touched by an angel. Why did she have to strap a board on her feet and hang out with a bunch of pot smokers? Why couldn't it be enough to just play?

I was still thinking things over on the way to school the next morning. I wanted to talk with the butterfly-happy Tay who loved hockey and didn't do drugs. She'd understand about playing in the snow, why it made me feel all happy and kind of revved up and wild, like I used to get, and Mom would say get out of the house, I was driving her nuts. Did we really have to give that up just because we were old enough to drive?

I found Tay in the Commons, slouched in a corner

with her feet up and her eyes closed. I grabbed the toe of her shoe and wiggled it.

"Hey Taylorini. How was the party?"

She didn't open her eyes. She grinned and said, "Fantastic. I'm still trying to recover."

"Well, recover quick," I said. "Bell's gonna ring in about two minutes."

She swung around and sat up.

"It would've been even better if you'd come," she said. "Maxie, there are some wild people in the snowboarding world. And you know what?"

I shook my head.

"I tried E," she whispered.

"Ecstasy? Tay, people die from that stuff."

"I know, I know," she said, waving her hand at that. "Only if you're stupid. I was careful, I got it from Jonathan at work. Max, you can't believe, it feels like, like, like delicious. Like everything good just dripping all over you at once, I mean, my face is kinda sore from smiling so much."

She closed her eyes and smiled some more.

"Hey Tay," I said. "Do you remember that butterfly? The blue one?"

"Of course. I'm going to get a tattoo of it on my eighteenth birthday. On my shoulder. What made you think about that?"

"You know the day after we went snowboarding?"

"Oh my god, that's right. I never got a chance to tell you about it. That's when I met Vanessa, this friend of Sam's. You'd really like her, Maxie. She was at the New

Year's party too, I told her all about you."

I opened my mouth to talk, but Tay kept going.

"She went to art school for a year, but then she dropped out and started teaching snowboarding. She teaches in Lake Tahoe and she says they go boarding in tank tops and shorts. I'd introduce you but she flew back yesterday."

"But Tay, you know that day when we got all that new snow?"

The bell rang and Tay looked at the ceiling and sighed.

"I don't know how long I can keep this up."

"Keep what up? What are you talking about?"

"Don't get that panicked look," she said, picking up her bag. "I'm not going to drop out or anything. Not this week anyway."

I opened my mouth to try again, but then decided against it. Playing in the snow with Rick Nash didn't stand up to Vanessa the snowboarding dropout.

When I got to chemistry fourth period, Rick lit up like he'd just gotten plugged into a socket. He had a new green sweater on, and it matched his eyes exactly. It hung funny on him, though. I couldn't figure how he did it—he had expensive clothes, but they all looked a bit wrong. On someone else, the sweater would have been fine.

"So?" he said. "How's the new year so far?"

"It's all right. I rang it in with Ben and Jerry."

"Those guys get around," he said. "They came by my place for a few hours, too. I finally had to send them home."

"Why, what were they doing?"

"It was the cows, B & J left them in the front yard and they were disturbing the peace. Mooing and all."

Patterson started rattling on about our next lab, but I didn't care. I ripped out a new piece of paper.

Let's do a Nash and Hawke mousetrap, I wrote. *Give me a diagram, something to start with.*

He stared at the note for a long time. Then he looked up at me. Then back at the note. He squinted at it like he was trying to crack the code. Finally he wrote back:

No mousetraps for me. I've given them up. Call it a New Year's Resolution.

I gave him the question eyebrows. He grabbed the notepaper back:

Knock knock.

Who's there?

Howie.

Howie who?

Howie gonna do this lab right if we don't pay attention?

CHAPTER 15

January eighteenth was my birthday and I woke to the smell of waffles. Mom and Dad sang and made a fuss over me and hinted around about the presents I could expect at dinner. A whole sky full of snow had fallen during the night, and we flipped the TV on just in case they decided to call school off. They didn't, but Dad gave me a ride so I wouldn't have to wade five miles uphill both ways through six feet of snow like he had to when he was a kid.

I got there a good half-hour before the first bell. Starting in seventh grade, Tay always decorated my locker. She outdid herself every year, finding good cartoon cards, *Far Side* and *Peanuts* mostly, and taping them up all over my locker door.

I scanned the hallway and kept checking over my shoulder. She usually planted herself somewhere unexpected and then jumped out to scream happy birthday and scare the life half out of me. No sign of her in the Commons, on the stairway, or down the rows of lockers.

Not even down my row. My locker was completely bare.

I'd only seen her once over Christmas break, and since New Year's she'd been spending the weekends snowboarding with Sam and his crowd so I only saw her at school. But we hadn't been fighting—I'd thought things were fine. It never came into my head that she'd blow off my birthday. Not once.

I moved forward slowly, hoping she was going to jump out from behind the lockers and blast me with a can of Silly String. She didn't. I stood alone in the hall and faced the bare gray metal. I put my fingers on the dial and turned my combo slowly. Eleven. Fourteen. Thirty. I pulled the latch up and opened the door, and my locker hissed.

Something inside flared, and I jumped back. Smoke came out, and the smell of sulfur, and a wave of panic rolled through my chest. But then I saw the cupcake.

It sat there on the shelf, spitting sparks. A lit sparkler was stuck in the frosting, a fizzling hissing birthday candle. Like the Fourth of July in my locker. The end of the sparkler drooped, glowing red as it burned down. It sizzled and spit and finally went out.

When I reached for it, I found the wires up the side, wrapped around a wooden match attached to the sparkler. The wires were duct-taped to the ceiling and ran down to a square battery that sat on top of my stacked books on the floor of the locker. Definitely not Tay's work.

Under the battery was an envelope:

Maxie Hawke

Rick's writing. As if anyone else I knew could figure

out a setup like that. I ripped open the envelope. The front of the card inside was a portrait, a guy's face. I knew it was some famous artist but I didn't know who. It was all different strokes of color and dabs of light making a circle around his head like a halo. I read the inside:

Requesting permission to act as tour guide in a purely platonic and non-date-like fashion for the birthday queen at the van Gogh exhibit at the art museum sometime this weekend. R. Nash.

I stood there staring at the card until the bell rang. I couldn't think of any really good reason to say no, and I wasn't even sure I wanted to. If it turned out to be half the fun that shoveling snow was, it would beat the heck out of sitting home alone or following Tay out to the Land of Snowboard. I put the cupcake back in the locker, picked up my books, and went down to the Commons to look for Tay.

She didn't show all morning, not even for English third period. I kept checking my cell for messages between classes, but there weren't any.

In chemistry, Rick acted all amazed about the cupcake and wondered who could have done a thing like that. He did admit to leaving the card in my locker, and we decided to go on Saturday afternoon. The way he acted about the cupcake reminded me a bit of the way he'd acted about the purple bangs in chemistry, and I took some double looks at him during class. Gym stink-bomb? Football game lights? No doubt he could have done all those things, but would he? No. Yes.

Should I ask him? That look I thought he'd shot me on dance night flashed through my head. No. Definitely not asking.

I took the cupcake with me to lunch and went over to our usual table, hoping Tay would show for the afternoon. Instead, Sean and Dex came weaving through the crowd and sat down on either side of me.

They sang low, not loud enough to make everyone turn around and look.

"Happy birthday to you. Happy birthday to you. Happy birthday, dear Maxie. Happy birthday to you. And many more. On Channel Four. And Frankenstein on Channel Nine. And Good 'n Plenty on Channel Twenty. And a big fat lady on Channel Eighty. And Eminem on Channel Ten. And Gilbert Grape on Channel Eight. And..."

They would have kept trading off rhymes all afternoon if I hadn't waved my hands and stopped them.

"All right, all right, all right," I said. "Enough already."

"Hey, a cupcake," said Dex. "You got more?"

"Where's Tay?" asked Sean.

"I don't know," I said. "She's not here today."

"On your birthday? Man, she'd better be dying sick in the bed if she's gonna miss your birthday."

"What are you doing here, anyway?" I asked. "Why aren't you in class?"

"For my favorite cousin's birthday? I can show up late for once."

"You gonna eat that cupcake?" asked Dexter.

"Listen to him," said Sean. "You'd think he had nothing on his mind but that cupcake, you'd never guess at the sensitive genius beneath."

"Some sensitive geniuses like cupcakes," said Dex.

"Well eat something else," I said. "My birthday, my cupcake. Go find your own food."

"You want anything?" he asked, standing up.

Sean and I shook our heads, and Dexter got in line.

"You okay?" Sean asked.

"I guess," I said. "I can't believe Tay didn't even call or anything. I just checked my messages. Do you think she's really sick? Like, dying or something?"

"She better be, that's all I can say. Hey listen, I really do have to get going to class. I just wanted to, you know."

"I know," I said. "Thanks."

He got up and left as Dex was coming back. The look that passed between them, I didn't see how everyone in the school could help but know.

Dex sat down across from me. We hadn't really talked since the dance in October. I studied him as he shoveled in the mac and cheese.

"Were you always popular?" I asked. "You were always picked first for kickball, right?"

"Yeah," he said. "But it's not really me, you know, that's popular. That was just about wanting me on their team. Still is, I think. But me, Dexter, none of them even know me."

"Don't you worry about it? I mean, what's going to happen when people find out you're not what they think?"

"I worry about it some," he said. "But then I figure, it's just high school. Even if the bottom falls out of the whole thing, so what? I'll be gone in five months."

"Then what?"

"I don't know," shrugged Dex. "I think I'm going to the U of M, and I was going to live at home for a year, but now I'm not so sure."

He put down his fork and shook his head.

"What's wrong?" I asked.

"I don't know," he said. "The bottom dropping out. It never goes like you think it's going to."

I watched him, waiting. Seemed like he was going to say something real. Since Tay had gone zipping off on her snowboard, I didn't get to hear much real.

"Sean said you busted him on the white privilege thing," said Dex. "What'd you use, some kind of white-people code? I couldn't even get him to listen about it."

"I used cousin code," I said. "But I hadn't ever thought about it either, like, I never once wondered about what it's like for Donovan at the Grands'."

"It's probably fine. I was fine at my mom's family's when I was a kid. It wasn't till I got older that I started noticing things. Anyway, whatever you said to Sean got him to shut up long enough to hear me. I couldn't handle it, fighting with him and my dad at the same time."

"How's that going with your dad? Sean said he eased off a little."

"I guess it's better," said Dex. "He's into a big Don't

Ask Don't Tell thing. And my mom went dashing off to a PFLAG meeting. It's like, one's as bad as the other."

"Seems like that's good," I said. "Her doing the PFLAG thing."

"No, it's not. Because they're both making it all about, oh, Dexter's gay, and that's not the point. Sean's the point. I mean, I want to have him over for dinner, maybe hang out at my house sometimes, but neither of them gives a rat's ass about Sean. It's all about, if Dexter's really gay, what do we do about it? And I think, forget about gay or not, who cares? The point is that I'm in love with Sean, even when he's being a Grade A butthead. Why can't it be about that?"

"It should be," I said. "Nobody in our family cares about the gay thing one way or the other. Maybe they cared with Uncle Max way back when, but that was a long time ago. Now it's just oh, Sean's boyfriend has such good manners, isn't that great."

"Yeah, see? My parents don't care if Sean has the manners of a hog, they've only met him once for like two minutes. I wish I could talk to my dad about the race stuff, he's dealt with it all, but forget that, to him it'd just be another reason to get on me about my bad choices. He thinks I'm not thinking about anything, but I'm thinking so hard it makes my head hurt."

He looked down.

"Sorry," he said. "I mean, sorry to get all heavy on you. It's just, I don't have anyone to talk to about this except Sean and I don't want it in our way all the time. Sometimes I want to go out and have fun and not always be dealing."

"Talk to me whenever you want," I said. "I don't have any great ideas, but I'll listen."

"Thanks." Dexter gave me a sort of sad little smile.

I took the knife from his tray and cut the cupcake, and gave him half.

"Rick gave it to me," I said.

"Nash?"

"Yup. He wired it in my locker with a sparkler on top. So I open my locker, and bang, the fuse lights and there it is, all lit up and sparking away."

"That's pretty elaborate."

"I know. But you know, I don't think it was that hard for him to do. He's really smart."

"Yeah, he's in my AP calc class and he blows everyone away in there. You don't suppose he made this himself? This is one good cupcake."

I broke my half off a little piece at a time. The chocolate frosting stood about two inches high, and the yellow cake part was nice and moist. I thought about asking Dex what he thought about the other stuff, the stink bomb and everything, but I didn't. He had enough on his mind.

"So are you two, you know...?"

"No," I said, licking frosting off my fingers. "We're just friends."

"If there's anyone who could use a friend it's that guy. Hey, you got some frosting—"

He pointed to the corner of his mouth.

"Thanks," I said, grabbing my napkin.

"Well, I should get going," he said, getting up. "Happy birthday."

He wove between tables to the garbage can, and kids yelled to him and slapped his hand as he walked by. I'd always seen him that way—popular, beautiful, friendly. He was so much more than that, though. I liked the way he'd acted about Rick. No smirks or eye-rolling, even when he asked if we were going out. Like Rick was just a regular guy.

That night at dinner, Mom was lighting up the birthday candles when the doorbell rang. I went to answer it and Tay stood there in her snowboarding gear, holding a bright blue envelope. I opened the storm door and leaned on it, hunching against the cold.

"Hey Maxie. Happy birthday."

"You went boarding," I said, rubbing my arms to stay warm. "That's where you've been all day."

"That's right," she said, grinning. "I spent your birthday in perfect powder, celebrating. I even hollered your name from the top of the chairlift."

"You couldn't call?" I said, sounding a lot like my mother.

"I can't get a signal there. But hey, I was thinking about you all day."

"Right. Thanks for the thought."

"Well," she said.

I didn't move to let her in. The cold wind whipped around between us and I shivered.

"Well. Um, happy birthday then."

She held the envelope out. I looked at it.

"Is that a birthday card?" I asked.

"What do you think?"

"I think it's weak. Why even bother?"

"Geez Max, lighten up. What's your problem?"

"You're fired," I said.

Tay half-smiled but I wasn't kidding. Instead of taking the card, I stepped back and let the storm door close between us. She dropped her hand to her side and we looked at each other through the glass. She cocked her head a little, waiting for me to open the door. When I didn't, she turned and walked away.

CHAPTER 16

I'd completely let go of Tay's long cold-shoulder treatment in November. I'd been a good sport the day of that snowboarding lesson when she left me on my butt. I'd put up with her going on and on about Sam and his coolio college dropout friends, I'd looked the other way that day she got stoned at school, and I'd even let go of all the times she was "too busy" to call. In fact, I'd spent more than four years glossing over Tay's moods and gaps, her occasional nastiness or neglect. But this was different. This was too much. She must be punished.

The rest of the week I took a bag lunch and ate in the gym. I sat up high on the bleachers and did homework or watched sophomore boys play basketball. Tay could try sitting alone in the Commons for a few days and see how she liked it. I didn't need her. I had plans for the weekend. I'd be way too busy to sit around wondering when she would call to apologize.

I fidgeted around the house Saturday until Rick showed at eleven. I changed clothes three times—I didn't want to look like I was trying to look good. He'd been very clear about the non-date status of this get-together and I wanted to make sure it stayed that way. When the Explorer pulled up out front I was waiting at the door with my jacket on.

Once I got in and we both said hi and how you doing, I couldn't think of anything else to say. He turned up the music, Pink Floyd.

"What kind of music do you like?" he asked.

"Oh, lots of different stuff." Mostly I liked whatever happy boppy pop tunes were out at the time, but I wasn't going to tell him that.

"I've got classic rock, some rap, jazz, blues, classical—your pick."

"You pick," I said, glad now that I hadn't said something stupid. "Too many choices for me."

"Okay, I'll leave it on shuffle."

The music filled the empty space around us and saved me from trying to make conversation.

We checked our coats at the museum entrance, and he insisted on paying my admission. I let him, seeing as how it was a birthday present. We wandered around, not exactly together but not exactly apart, either. We finally came together in front of a print of van Gogh's self-portrait, the same one that was on the birthday card Rick gave me.

"I'd love to see the original of this," he said. "This guy was a crazy genius."

I stood with my arms across my chest and looked at the portrait in front of me. It was so different from what I did. I liked simple lines. He didn't have one line in there. It was all dabs of color hitched together to make shapes, so complicated, and yet it was still the same thing. A face. Only because of the dabs and the color, you could see underneath the face, to the layers of everything he ever had been and everything he might want to be.

"So Maxie, have you been taking art classes all along?" Rick asked.

"No."

"Why not?"

"I don't do real art," I said. "Just cartoons."

"But the way you whipped out that winged pig, boom, there's a pig on the paper. Not just any old pig, either, that was a live, snorting pig. I almost had to swat at it to keep it from buzzing in my ears."

"That's not real art," I said, laughing as he swung his long arms around over his head. "Not like this stuff."

"Who says one's more real than the other? Art's supposed to make you feel something, right?"

"I guess."

"Well, your pig made me feel something. So it's art."

"Tell that to Mr. Heiden," I said. "I took art freshman year and I got a C. You know how embarrassing that was?"

"Well, then Heiden's an idiot. Even the Nash & Hawke mousetraps were art."

"Ha," I said, shaking my head. "Not even creative. You did all the thinking, I just drew what you said. I missed out on the creative gene."

"You're wrong, Maxie. Creativity, it's not just making stuff up. It's about getting it down on paper in a way that people can see."

He pointed at van Gogh's self-portrait.

"Like look, imagine this guy looking in a mirror. He didn't make up a new guy. He just drew what he saw. It's real. You do the same thing. You look at something or hear something and wham, you put it on paper and I'm going yeah, that's what I meant."

He took a step back, still looking at the portrait.

"Like with the mousetraps, you didn't just put down the mechanics. You made the whole idea jump off the page. You even do it with our lab reports. I think it's cool, and I think it's art."

I kept looking into the layers of color while he talked. That way I didn't have to try to say thank you or no it's not art or anything else. I could just listen.

He kicked his foot sideways into mine.

"Come on," he said. "There's a lot more to see."

We moved on to another wing of the museum and found a series of oil paintings of kids. We stopped in front of a picture full of soft blues and tans, a boy and girl making a sand castle with the ocean behind them.

"Don't you wish we could go back to stuff like that?" asked Rick.

"You have no idea," I said.

We walked on, browsing through the rooms, stopping here and there.

"Who's your favorite cartoonist?" he asked me.

"Charles M. Schulz. My dad used to read to me from *Peanuts Treasury* at bedtime when I was a kid. It was my favorite."

"Why?"

"The way he took big world things, you know, and made it about a kite or a baseball game, or a conversation between a beagle and a bird. Just a few simple lines and a few words, he got it all."

"I never thought about it," said Rick. "But I think you're right. I'll have to brush up on my Charlie Brown."

"I'd love to do what he did—get it all down in four simple squares. He was the master."

"Maybe," he said. "But I'd take that winged pig over Woodstock any day."

He swatted at the air again, and I laughed out loud. It was fun being away from school and everyone I knew. It felt a lot like fifth grade, not some boy-girl thing, but just friends. He was easy to talk to. He made me think, and he made me laugh. I liked him.

When Monday rolled around I didn't pack a lunch. I wanted a hot lunch, and besides, I'd made my point by staying away from the Commons the past few days. So I stood in the lunch line and got a plate of spaghetti. When I came out of the line, Tay was sitting at our usual spot. She waved at me—and it wasn't the wave of someone who knew she'd been punished and was sorry. It made me mad all over again.

Three girls from Civics sat over to my right. I considered sitting with them. I could do that. There was no law against it. I glanced over at Tay again. She put her hands out in an exaggerated shrug, like hey, what's up?

A guy bumped me from behind.

"Oops, sorry," he said, and the girl with him giggled.

The Civics girls looked up. They giggled too, and that was more than I could handle. I walked over to our table and set my tray down across from Tay.

She started yammering away about Sabrina Granquist's new hair color.

"Tay."

She kept talking, like I hadn't even said anything.

"Tay!" I said it louder, waving my hands at her.

"What?"

"Don't you have something to say to me?"

"Like what?"

She looked at me so blank-faced, so stoned-brained, I finally got it. This was the new non-hockey Tay. I might have been a little nervous when it came to telling the old Tay about going to the museum with Rick— ready to defend him and take a hard joke or two. But this Tay? I wasn't telling her anything. About anything.

After school I dug my colored markers out from the bottom of my desk. They were still brand new—I hardly ever used color. Pencil, pen, maybe charcoal. But that van Gogh portrait, it cracked open something new in my head. The birthday card from Rick was still on my dresser and I stared at it for a while. I picked up a marker and started moving my hand on the page. While it moved I ran memories around in my mind: knock-knock jokes, playing in the snow, and the scary Rick-eyes from the pep rally. Conversations and chemistry labs, the winged pig and mousetraps. I didn't think. I just let my hand move across the page, this way and that. I picked up different markers, made lines, and put them down again.

When the page was full of lines and color, I propped the sketchbook on my pillow and backed away. The sun came through the window and shone on it, and it was different from anything I'd ever drawn before. It wasn't a cartoon, but it wasn't not a cartoon. It was lines, but it was more than lines. It wasn't quite Rick and it wasn't quite Roddy, but it was some mix of the two of them and maybe something else.

I'd never signed any of my drawings. I printed my name on assignments for art class, or put "Love, Maxie" at the bottom of pictures I drew for people, but that was separate, and different. Signing on purpose, as part of the drawing, that was for art.

I picked up a pen, took a deep breath, and in the bottom corner of the picture, interlacing with the edges of lines and color, I wrote: *M. Hawke*

I carefully pulled the page out of my sketchbook and took it to school with me the next day. I folded it over once and slid it through the vent of Rick's locker.

When Rick came into chemistry fourth period, he smacked his books down onto the table and pointed at me.

"You," he said. "You just lost any right you ever had to say you're not an artist."

"You like it?" I asked.

"Jesus, Maxie," he said, shaking his head. "I don't know how you did that."

I didn't know either. I'd never done anything like it before.

CHAPTER 17

The next weekend, Rick and I went to an artsy little theater tucked away behind a grocery store. We saw a Chinese film and went out for Indian food after. I'd never had Indian food and I'd never had a conversation like that. Not about school or our families, but about taking ideas or an image and making it into something other people can relate to, no matter who they are or what language they speak. It was fun in a way that I never knew talking could be fun. I ended up with his number in my cell.

Over the next few weeks my life outside of school morphed into a new normal. When my phone rang it wasn't Tay. It was Rick. We started going to a little coffee shop way over on the north side. We drank hot chocolate and wrote up our lab reports together, or he read and I sketched. I skipped going out to the Grands' when Rick got tickets to an afternoon play. He didn't try to hold my hand or gaze into my eyes and we never went anywhere we were likely to be seen by kids from school.

We were just pals, Maxie and Roddy again, only better.

Rick took my drawing seriously. He told me exactly what he liked and why. Sometimes he asked questions. He didn't say anything was bad or stupid or wrong; he just said he didn't understand this expression or that movement. He made me want to do the drawing again, work on it, make it better.

Tay had always liked my cartoons and my cousins loved them, especially when they were in them. My parents put my drawings on the fridge and bought me art supplies, but even they had never poked around under the surface the way Rick did. Through his eyes, I started seeing my art in a whole different way, and I liked it.

I didn't tell Tay one thing about Rick. She never asked what I was up to on the weekends and as far as I was concerned, she didn't deserve to know. All she cared about was the ten-day forecast.

I continued to sit with her at lunch when she was there, but she missed a lot of school. She came down with a mystery disease every time we got a new snow. Sean wasn't around much either. He had picked up another class at the university for second semester, so he was only at school for two hours in the morning. He'd quit coming out to the Grands' for Sunday dinners altogether. Dexter started turning up at lunchtime, and I ate with him almost as often as I did with Tay. It was nice—I could talk to him about hanging out with Rick, and it was no big deal.

"So did you do anything exciting over the weekend?" he asked the Monday after Valentine's Day.

The truth was I'd worried about it the whole week before. Going somewhere with Rick on Valentine's weekend, that seemed date-like no matter what. All the perfectly good excuses I'd invented went unused, though. He didn't suggest anything for the weekend and didn't even call.

"Nope. Just went out to the Grands' and played games and made a snow fort. We can't all have exciting love lives the way you do."

Dexter grinned.

"Hey look, you're actually blushing! I don't think I've ever seen you blush before."

"I save it for special occasions," he said. "So how come I never see you and Rick hanging together at school? Where's he go for lunch?"

"I don't know."

Dexter gave me a long look that made me twitch.

"We get along best when it's just the two of us," I explained. "Even back when we were little kids. Things are—I don't know—they're different at school."

Dexter kept looking.

"It's not just me," I pointed out. "I don't even see him outside of chemistry, so how would I know what he does? Besides, you and Sean don't hang out together at school."

Anyone else would have said it right away, but not Dexter. He just looked at me.

"Okay, so I don't want to deal with the way people clown on him," I said. "I don't like it."

"Me neither," he said, still looking at me. Then he shook his head and looked out across the Commons, and I swear I felt him gently take the hook out of the roof of my mouth. "I can't wait to get out of this high-school game. I am over it."

"You've only got a few months left," I said, squirming away free but not feeling any better about myself. "Then you're done."

"I hope I like the next game better. Meanwhile, I've got calc."

We got up and dumped our trays together and I headed for my locker, still thinking about the things Dexter hadn't said. He seemed like such an easy-breezy guy on the surface, but he didn't miss much.

Dexter's look stuck with me over the next couple of weeks, poking at me. Rick was a great friend to me. He didn't show any signs of hitting on me or trying to make our friendship into a dating thing. Avoiding him at school was wrong. It was sixth grade all over again, no matter how I tried to make it about something else.

Friday in chemistry, he seemed particularly down. Not in a biting-on-tinfoil way like he did sometimes—just sad. He didn't even take notes during Patterson's lecture. He sat there staring off into space, his pen lying on clean white notebook paper. I left chemistry thinking that if I were any kind of friend at all, I'd ask him what was wrong.

So when the last bell rang, I grabbed my jacket and rushed down the stairs to the basement row of lockers where I'd met him that day after the pep rally. I spotted him putting books in his backpack.

"Hey Rick," I called.

He turned around and I waved at him.

"What are you doing now?" I asked.

He looked up and down the hall, and back to me.

"Nothing, why?" He seemed puzzled.

"Do you want to go get some pizza or something?"

You would've thought I'd offered him a gourmet five-star dinner and a ride in Sean and Dexter's limo to get there.

"Sure, that sounds great! I know a place out on the west side, we could go there..."

We went out the side door. Winter had been sitting back on its haunches for a few days, and spring was trying to move in but wasn't quite getting anywhere. The snow was hard and dirty, hunkered in big frozen piles around the edges of the lot. The air had a damp chill.

"Sure feels cold, for not being very cold," said Rick.

"I know," I said, zipping my jacket all the way up. "Feels colder now than it did back in January when it was below zero for five years."

We'd been slow moving out of the building, so most of the cars were already gone from the lot. Rick's Explorer was parked alone over in the far corner. As we came close to it, Rick suddenly stopped dead, and I ran

right into him. There was no give when I bumped him;
he was stone rigid. I looked where he was looking.

Someone had keyed all the way around, a harsh dig
in the blue paint. Big jagged letters spread across the
driver's side door.

FAGGOT

The word smacked me in the face. I looked at Rick.

His face was still set, but waves of heat radiated off
of him. He stared at the word with his laser-eyes and I
could almost imagine the whole thing blowing up, just
from that look. I was scared to say anything or even to
move. For a long moment I stood there, my stomach
lurching around somewhere near my tonsils.

Then it was like someone threw a switch inside of
him. The color in his face eased off, his body relaxed,
and he looked at me with a sad sort of smirk.

"Well look at that, the canaille have been howling in
the parking lot today."

"The what?"

"Canaille. Masses, rabble, riffraff, mob. The pack
of howling dogs."

He shook his head and walked around, touching the
gouges and grooves in the smooth, recently washed and
waxed paint. No salt stains on this car. I followed him,
horrified.

"You shouldn't touch it, Rick. I think they can get
fingerprints off it. You should call and report it, right
away."

"Ah, Maxie. I know you live in that world, but I

don't. In my world, you club one dog down and a thousand more rise to take its place."

Then he turned and looked at me hard. Not the full lasers, but enough to make me step back.

"No reporting."

"All right," I said, but it wasn't all right.

"I'm afraid I'll have to bow out of the pizza party. I have some other things to attend to."

"What other things?" I asked. "You're not going to do something stupid, are you?"

"What do you think I would do? Some spontaneous and pointless form of retribution? That's not my style. I'll just go find some sedulous soul at a body shop who can set this right in a hurry. If my father sees it, he'll be completely unhinged. And if you don't mind, I'll ask you to get home under your own power. I doubt you want to be seen in this, anyway."

"Rick, are you sure you don't want me to..."

"Absolutely sure," he said.

I stood there as he got in and started the engine. He lowered the window.

"There is one thing you can do for me, Maxie."

"What?"

"You can completely forget about this. Pretend it never happened. Okay?"

I said okay. Like I was doing him some big favor.

CHAPTER 18

The next day I woke to a fluffy, gentle-flake snow. I lay in bed and watched it fall. The house was quiet. My bed was warm.

The doorbell rang and I waited for someone to answer it. It rang again, so I got up and shivered over to the window. Rick was parked out front. He must have found his body-shop guy, because the markings on his door were gone.

I pulled on sweats over my pajamas and clipped down the stairs. Was he okay? He'd never shown up without calling before. Maybe something horrible had happened. Maybe his dad had kicked him out.

"Knock knock," he said, knocking on the doorjamb as I opened the door.

His shoulders were curled in and he didn't look up. I stepped back, holding the storm door open so he could come in. He didn't move.

"Knock knock," he said. He was quiet and insistent, looking at his feet.

"Who's there?"

"Despair."

"Despair who?" I whispered.

"Despair shovel's fine with me. You can use the good one."

He brought his head up and grinned big at me.

"I know," he said. "Bad joke. But look, it's pretty outside. Ah, sorry, I should have called first."

"No no no," I said. I was so relieved that the despair was a joke, I was falling all over myself. "Come on in. Sit down. There's the remote, watch cartoons or something. I'll just be a few minutes."

He stepped inside and I ran upstairs. I brushed my teeth and washed my face and tried to do something about my hair. When I got back downstairs, Rick was still standing in the doorway with his jacket and boots on.

"So, are you ready to shovel?" he asked.

"Right now?" I said. "It's still snowing too hard. We'd just have to do it again later."

"Oh."

I never saw anyone look so disappointed over not getting to shovel snow.

"If you want to hang around for a minute," I said, "I'll make us some hot chocolate. I owe you from before anyway, and maybe by then it'll stop snowing."

"Where's your parents?" he asked, looking around.

"I don't know. I just got up."

"Sorry."

"Don't be," I said, heading for the kitchen. "I was

awake, I was just lying around. Oh look, here's a note on the table. They went out to Rocklin Park for the day. Cross-country skiing. I'll get the hot chocolate going."

I put the teakettle on and came back to lean in the doorway.

"So your parents actually go skiing together?" he asked as he unlaced his boots.

"Yeah. They're really into it. They used to try and drag me along, but I think they have more fun without me."

"Huh," said Rick. "I can't imagine my parents having fun, with or without me."

I went back into the kitchen and pulled out a couple of mugs and packages of hot chocolate. I wondered how he was doing about the keying, if his dad had found out about it. I sure wasn't going to bring it up, but the least I could do was make him some extra good hot chocolate.

I poured mix into the mugs and rooted around the freezer looking for Cool Whip, but we didn't have any. I glanced out into the living room. Rick was on the couch. He looked over his shoulder at me and half-smiled. One thing, he did have pretty eyes. Sometimes when I looked at them, I could see someone good-looking in there trying to get out. Maybe in about ten years, when his acne cleared up and he started some dot-com and became a millionaire.

The kettle rattled and whistled on the burner, and I poured water into the mix, topping things off with miniature marshmallows. I carried the mugs out, gave him one, and sat on the other end of the couch, curling my feet up under me.

Rick turned and looked at me with an extra-serious face.

"So Maxie," he said, and those two words carried about fifty pounds each.

"What?"

"There's something I've been wanting to tell you."

His ears went red and I quit breathing.

"This last month or so? While we've been, you know, spending some time together?"

His face blotched up, and I started to sweat. It was like sitting in the back seat of a car you thought was parked and all of a sudden it starts rolling.

"Well, it's been..." He swirled the mug around. "It's been good. I mean, good, like, good. Like really good."

When he looked up at me, his eyes were so naked with everything—with little Roddy asking me to come over and me saying no, with the happy excitement of playing in the snow together, with the sadness in chemistry the day before and the way he lit up when he saw me in the hallway and the horrible shock of FAGGOT on his car door—all of that rushed out of his eyes on a river of feeling and washed away the fence I'd kept between us to hold him at a safe distance.

I set down my hot chocolate and moved over, and I put a hand on his knee, just to, I don't know. To tell Roddy, Rick, it was okay, I guess. That I was his friend,

I was there for him. It was the first time I'd touched him on purpose since the day I stuffed snow down his neck. He sucked in his breath, almost winced.

That suck of breath and the intensity of his liquid green eyes, they mixed together and shot out a jolt of something buzzy and warm. It ripped all the way through me, inside and out, a current of electric power and heat that I had no idea was in me or between us.

My hand shook as it moved up to his shoulder, and then his neck. He leaned into it, and all I could see were his eyes. Like they cancelled out everything. They came in closer, and he kissed me, and I kissed back.

It was nothing like the couple of stupid kisses I'd had before, with two mouths slopping around trying to feel something. This was different. Like he was saying something with his lips, sort of whispering in watercolor. Everything went soft and blurry, and I moved in closer.

I closed my eyes and drifted back and he moved with me, floating on that current of soft buzzy warmth. Then all at once, the lines sharpened and hardened. I was trapped under Rick and he was all over me, kissing me harder, pushing up against me. His hand started moving across my shirt, crawling up my ribs.

I wiggled and squirmed sideways and fell off the couch, and my head bounced on the floor. Rick's face appeared above me, eyes wide open. I was relieved and embarrassed and started giggling and couldn't stop. Rick's eyes narrowed into hard green lines. The same green lines I'd seen when he stared Lance down at the pep rally.

I stopped laughing.

"Hey, I'm sorry," I said. "I didn't mean to laugh. I just—it was funny—my head bounced."

He kept looking at me, and a cold shiver slid down my spine. Finally, he moved back. I got up and sat on the couch again, off in my own corner.

"Really," I said. "I'm sorry. I just—"

"Why did you touch me like that?"

He pinned me in the corner with those green slits.

"Because you looked so sad, and you know, yesterday, and—"

"What?" he yelled. The way he looked, it was like I'd just punched him hard. "You did this because you felt *sorry* for me?"

"No, no, it's not like that at all. Listen Rick, your friendship means a lot to me and—"

"My friendship?" He jerked up off the couch. "My friendship means a lot to you? What's that supposed to mean? No, don't. Don't even say it."

He spun away from me, snatching his jacket from the end of the couch. He rammed his feet in his boots without lacing them and left in a whoosh of cold air and a slam of the door. I knew I should tell him to stop, wait, that's not what I meant, but everything happened so fast and besides, I was still so surprised by the kiss and all those feelings before and after that I didn't know what to say even if he did stop.

So I let him go.

CHAPTER 19

I sat on the couch for a long time after Rick left, staring out the window. I glanced at the clock. It wasn't even ten yet. In less than an hour, everything had spun from asleep to hot chocolate to watercolors to laser eyes. Like I was Jordan Feltz flicking his ears.

I went out later and shoveled the snow by myself. Finally, on Sunday night, after hashing through everything in my head about ten million times, I sent Rick an email.

hey rick, i'm really sorry about what happened yesterday. i know u got mad when i said that about friendship, but i didn't mean it the way u think. we should talk. cu in chem 2morro.

I stressed all morning about what we'd say to each other, but he didn't show up on Monday. Or Tuesday. By Wednesday I was so nervous about seeing him again that I thought I was going to throw up after third period. He still didn't show. That night I called his cell and jiggled my foot up and down while it rang. His voicemail picked up, and I tried to sound casual.

"Hey Rick, this is Maxie. Are you okay? Are you sick or something? Um, well, I was just wondering. Talk to you later."

Thursday morning, I had a return message on my cell.

"Maxie. Don't call me anymore. I don't need your pity and I don't need your 'friendship' either. Find someone else to feel sorry for."

His voice dripped with the kind of acid you're not supposed to handle without gloves and safety goggles. It made me want to pour disinfectant through my phone. It was a lousy way to start the day, and I was more nervous than ever about chemistry. He'd show up there eventually, and now it looked like it'd be ugly when he did.

He didn't, though. Tay didn't show up at school that day either, so I took my lunch alone to our corner table and faced the wall.

A hand fell on my shoulder and I almost spit out the first bite of my grilled cheese sandwich. I jerked around.

"Dex! You scared me to death."

"Why so jumpy?" he asked, coming around the table to sit across from me.

"You don't want to know."

"Sure I do."

"Rick and I had a bad scene and he hasn't been to school since."

"I noticed he wasn't in calc," said Dex. "What happened?"

"It's kind of hard to explain," I said. "I guess the main point is, he kissed me, and then the whole thing got messy."

"Uh-oh. How messy?"

"Pretty bad. He thinks I laughed at him, and he thinks I only kissed him because I felt sorry for him. I did laugh and it did sort of start because I felt sorry about something that happened, but that's not the whole picture. He took off before I had a chance to explain anything, and I haven't seen him since. But now listen to this."

I pulled up the voicemail and let Dex listen, watching his face as the lunch noise clattered on around us.

"Whoa," he said, pulling away from the phone like it hurt his ear. "He's mad, all right."

"I know. He's just got it wrong, that's all, but how am I supposed to explain if he won't talk to me?"

"How wrong is he?" asked Dex. He chugged his milk, set the carton down, and gave me the straight-eye. "Would you kiss him again?"

I met Dexter's eyes and held them. They weren't clear green like Rick's. They hedged over into hazel. They flicked up as a Nerf football came flying past my ear. Dex caught it with a smack, right over his tray.

"Can't you see I'm busy?" he yelled, and he stood up

and flung it back.

Then he sat back down and looked at me.

"Would you?"

I squirmed. I had two answers, and neither of them was quite right.

"Maybe," I said, finally.

"Maybe?"

"It just happened so fast. I hadn't even thought about anything like that. Kissing or anything. Then all of a sudden, wham, we're kissing, and for a minute it seemed really good. Then things got kind of confused."

"Well, it sounds like you hurt him big-time. Maybe he's just got a hot temper and it'll all blow over. Leave him alone for a while and then see what's what."

"How long?"

"I don't know, Maxie," said Dex, standing and picking up his tray. "From the sounds of that voice mail, I wouldn't rush him any. Wait till he's cooled off some. He's gotta come back to school sometime. You're still lab partners, right?"

"As far as I know."

The bell rang, and I followed Dexter to the garbage can.

"So wait till he shows up in chemistry," he said, dumping his tray and reaching for mine. "When he does, be extra nice, and whatever you do, don't laugh at him."

"I know, I got it. Hey Dex—thanks."

"No charge," he said.

The football came flying at him as he walked away,

and he jumped to catch it. Something caught the corner of my eye and I looked up. Rick stood at the balcony railing, staring down at Dexter. He turned his head and watched as Dex walked around the corner to the stairway. Then he looked back at me.

Our eyes locked, just like they did that night at the dance. But this time, nobody walked between us to break the gaze. We just looked at each other until the bell rang. Then he turned away. The breath rushed out of me and my legs shook so hard I had to sit down.

Easy for Dex to say, be extra nice. But how could I be extra nice in the face of that? Whoever that guy was up there with the frozen green eyes, it wasn't the Rick I knew. It was someone I didn't want any part of.

The next day I saw his Explorer out in the lot and I was a nervous wreck by the time I got to fourth period. But he didn't show, and Ms. Patterson hooked me up to work with another lab team. At lunchtime I walked past the food line without stopping. My stomach was still chewing on itself. I sat down across from Tay.

"Why aren't you eating?" she asked.

The way she chowed into her pizza, it didn't look to me like she cared that much. I shrugged, and she shrugged back.

A bunch of freshman boys sat at the end of our table and started trying to out-burp each other. We turned away from them.

"Did you hear what happened to Rupert Findlay yesterday?" Tay asked around a mouthful.

"Who's Rupert Findlay?"

"The freshman kid with all the freckles."

"Oh yeah," I said, remembering the day about a million years ago when Jordan threw that kid up against the lockers. "What about him?"

The boys at the end of the table started talking back and forth over their burps, which didn't help my uneasy stomach.

"In P.E. second period, they tossed him outside butt-naked."

"They what?" I asked, my voice hiking up a few notes.

Tay nodded. "I guess they started messing with him, putting his clothes in the shower and stuff. One thing led to another, and the first thing you know they picked him up and dumped him outside, out that door by the locker room where you can go out but you can't come in. They left him out there squealing like a little pig on ice."

"How do you even know about this?" I asked.

"Eat me baby," said one of the boys over a burp, and they all snickered and another guy punched him in the arm.

I scowled at the burper and he hung his tongue out and made grabby motions with his hands. I turned my back on him.

"Joe Matthews was there," she said. "He told me about it in study hall."

"I thought Joe was an okay kid."

"He is. It wasn't his idea. He even kind of tried to

stop it, but you know how that stuff can snowball. Anyway, when they were carrying Rupert across the hall, someone saw them. You know who?"

I shook my head.

"Your pal Nash. He was getting something from his locker. And Joe, he figured them all being freshmen, Nash would break the whole thing up. You know what Nash did?"

She chomped through her pizza crust. My throat jammed like it had a glob of that crust stuck halfway down.

"Nothing," she said. "Not one thing. He looked straight at what was going on, and then he turned around and walked away. Can you believe that? Of all people, not to do something. Joe said he acted like he couldn't care less."

She finished off her pizza and waited for me to say something. When I didn't, she kept talking.

"So anyway, Joe felt bad and after the bell rang and everyone left, he got Rupert's clothes out of the shower for him. When he opened the door, Rupert was in a little wad there, he hadn't moved, he was just sitting there freezing and bawling."

"I tell you," she said, wiping her hands on a napkin, "I'm glad I'm not a guy. You gotta either be the rabbit or a hound, and if you won't be a hound, the other guys—whoa, whoa, Maxie, what's wrong?"

I felt the tears coming but I couldn't stop them. For a minute I thought I was going to hurl all over the table. If I'd eaten any lunch I probably would have. Whatever look was running across my face, it shook Tay right out of her too-cool-for-school attitude.

"Maxie, geez, what is it?"

I couldn't stop. The whole thing, the kissing and the blowup and the voicemail and walking on eggshells and tiptoeing around corners, it all came charging in and grabbed me and shook me around in its teeth and all I could do was flop back and forth in it like some kind of ragdoll.

I put my head down on the table. Tay leaned across and put a hand on my arm, and that made me cry even more. I was tired of the glass between me and Tay, too. I just wanted her to be my friend again.

"Max, come on, it's okay. He didn't get hurt or anything. Joe gave him his clothes before anyone even saw him."

"I don't feel good," I managed to say. "I think I'm sick."

"I've got my mom's car today. Do you want me drive you home?"

I nodded, but I wouldn't pick my head up. If I did, I'd have to see everything. I didn't want to see anything.

CHAPTER 20

Tay dropped me at home and I went right to bed. I woke up around nine that night feeling like I'd been swallowing razor blades. I kicked up a big fever and stayed wrapped in bed for most of the weekend. The best part about being sick was that I didn't have to figure anything out. Every time my mind started to churn around all that had happened and everything I should have or shouldn't have done, I went back to sleep.

My parents spoiled me rotten. Mom spent over an hour Saturday morning rubbing my temples and face. Dad read to me from his *Peanuts* book like I was four years old. It was good to feel crummy physically and have them be so nice to me without having to explain everything else I felt crummy about. I opened my mouth once to talk to Dad, but I was still so confused by it all I couldn't figure out what to say. So I closed my mouth and my eyes and went back to sleep.

By Sunday afternoon I didn't feel much better, but I wasn't technically sick anymore. The sun came pouring in my bedroom window, and I got up and stood in the rays, wrapped in a quilt. I put my face against the glass and looked down the street.

A blue Explorer was on the next block, coming my way.

My heart revved its nervous motor and I stepped back from the window so I couldn't be seen. The Explorer stopped at the stop sign, then crawled past our house. I shifted over a bit and watched as it rolled to the end of the block, turned right, and disappeared.

I didn't look out the window anymore.

Monday morning the sky was gray and cold and damp. The snow held on, dirty and icy. I trudged to school, still hacking up lung gunk from my cold. I kept an eye on the street, turning to look every time I heard a car. Rick driving by my house, I didn't like that. What if he turned into some kind of crazy stalker?

A few kids were hanging around in the Commons, but it was still early. The stairwell was empty as I went up, and the halls were quiet. I headed over to my locker, spun the combination and lifted the handle and

I jumped back against the opposite row. The locker door yawned open. My heart hammered like crazy, jumping all over the inside of my chest. My books had been dumped underneath, just like on my birthday. Something was on the top shelf, and it sure wasn't a cupcake. It was flat so I couldn't really see it. I took a step forward. Then another one. Nothing was hissing or burning. I stood on tiptoe.

It was a snapped mousetrap. The old-fashioned wooden kind. A folded piece of paper lay in its grip. I reached in, lifted the trap spring, and pulled the paper loose. My heart punched at my ribs like it was trying to get out.

I unfolded the paper. It was the picture I'd drawn of Rick. I turned it over, looking for a note. Nothing. I spun around, looking behind me. Then I put the picture back in my locker. I shut the door with both hands like maybe that would keep everything in there from coming out and getting me. Then I ran for the stairs. I didn't want to be in that empty hallway all by myself. I ran through the Commons, looking for Tay, and then busted out the door and whammed right into Dexter on his way in.

"Maxie! What's wrong?"

"It's Rick," I said. "He set up a mousetrap in my locker so it went off when I opened the door and it scared the crap out of me. It's creepy, Dex. Psycho creepy."

Dex put his arm around me and pulled me over against the wall.

"Hey, hey, come on. You're okay."

"What's up?" asked Sean, coming in behind Dexter.

"Rick's got her freaked out," said Dex. "He's acting kind of weird."

"No, Dex. Not 'kind of' weird. Psycho weird. The trap snapped on a picture I drew of him. What's that supposed to mean? Plus he knows how to do all kinds of stuff, batteries and explosions and what if, you know..."

"What trap?" asked Sean. "What picture?"

"Call him," said Dex, pulling his phone out of his pocket. "Right now. Call and find out where he is."

I stepped back, shaking my head. "Remember that voice mail?"

"Come on, Max. If you really think he's up to something that bad, you don't have time to fool around. Call him, or we go to the office and report it. Now."

No reporting. That's what Rick had said that day in the lot. But maybe I should have, what if he... I dug my own cell phone out of my bag, flipped it open, then stopped.

"What do I say?"

"Find out where he is."

I pulled up his number and hit talk. His phone rang once, twice, three times. I was opening my mouth to leave a message when he picked up.

"Maxie? Why are you calling me?" He sounded half-choked, like he was in the middle of swallowing a big chunk of meat.

"Rick? Where are you?"

He didn't answer.

"Rick, are you okay? Where are you?"

"Oh shit. Shit shit shit. I forgot about the trap."

He made a noise that could have been a sob. "That's it, isn't it? That's why you're calling."

"Rick, where are you?"

He didn't answer. Sean and Dex both had their eyes glued on me.

"I think he's crying," I whispered.

Sean's eyebrows went up.

"Find out where he is," whispered Dex.

"Rick!" I yelled into the phone. "Hey Rick! Where are you? Hey Rick!"

"Don't yell at me! I'm at the Motel 6, why, you want to do an interview?"

"What are you doing there?"

"Nothing, all right? I'm not doing a goddamn thing so go back to your happy life and leave me alone."

There was a clatter-crash and then nothing. I slid down the wall and sat on the floor. Sean and Dex squatted in front of me.

"Well?" said Dex. "What'd he say?"

"He's at a Motel 6."

I closed my eyes. I still didn't want to see anything, but now I couldn't help it.

"Why?" asked Sean. "What started all this?"

"Sean, just shut up a minute. Did he say anything else, Maxie?"

"He said go back to my happy life."

"Did he sound like, um, like he'd left something here or anything?"

"No," I said. "I don't think so."

The door swung open and a group of kids stepped

around us. Normal kids on their way to class. The guys
scooted out of the way, one on each side of me.

"I don't know what to do," I said in a tiny small
voice.

"We should go find him," said Dex. "Sounds like
he's in trouble."

"How? Motel 6, that could be anywhere."

"No, there aren't that many around," said Sean.
"I bet he's at that one out by the airport, right off the
freeway."

"Even if he is, how would I get there?" I asked.

"We'll drive you," said Dex. "If he's not there, we
can ask the clerk to call around and find where he is. If
he is there, we'll both be with you, and we can help you
figure out what to do."

"I'm not going anywhere until someone tells me
what's going on," said Sean.

"We'll tell you on the way. Maxie?
What do you say?"

What if I didn't go? What if I just
said never mind and turned around
and went to English? I'd sit through
that class, then another and another,
and then I'd go to chemistry and sit
next to his empty chair and...

"Okay," I said. "Let's go."

CHAPTER 21

Everything was gray. Highway, sky, clouds, naked trees. Tired snow piles with patches of dead grass showing through. Power lines, overpasses, and dirty, salt-streaked cars. No color anywhere. No color in what I told Sean, either. Hung out with Rick. Had a brief make-out scene. Laughed because I hit my head on the floor. He got hurt and stomped out. All the weirdness that followed.

I didn't talk about the watercolor whisper I'd felt when we first started kissing, that shining splash of goodness before everything exploded into bad. I didn't talk about the trip to the art museum or playing in the snow or the picture I'd drawn of him. I just gave the cold gray facts, then sat back and stared out the window.

We pulled up in the parking lot next to the Explorer, the only car in the lot. Dex turned off the engine and they waited for me to take the lead.

"Maybe this wasn't such a good idea," I said. "What if he's, you know, not stable or something?"

"From what you've said, he's not," said Sean. "But what are we going to do, leave him crying in the Motel 6?"

"Okay, but stay with me."

"Like Velcro," said Dexter, getting out of the car, and Sean and I followed.

Room 8, right in front of the Explorer, had its shades pulled.

"You think that's it?" I asked, knowing that it was. Every other room had open shades.

Dexter nodded, and I knocked. Nobody answered.

"Rick?" I said to the closed door. "Rick, it's me. Maxie."

I knocked again. The safety bolt slid, the doorknob turned, and the door opened just enough to unlatch. I waited, holding my breath. Sean reached over my head and nudged it inwards. The room was dark, the curtains pulled.

My eyes adjusted. Rick sat on the floor, leaning up against the far bed. He held his arms around himself in a funny way, like he had a stomachache. The whole left side of his face was blue and purple and swollen.

"Rick, what happened?" I gasped, stepping closer.

He put his hand up like a traffic cop and I stopped.

"Are you okay?"

He shook his head no.

"What are you doing here?" he asked, his voice missing a whole lot of air.

I looked back to where Sean and Dex stood in the doorway. Help, I said with my eyes. Sean took a step forward.

"Rick?" he said, flipping on the light.

Rick's head whipped up, his good eye narrowed.

"Turn off that light and get out of here, McGinnis," he said.

"Hey, sorry," Sean backed away, both hands up. "Sorry man. I didn't mean anything by it. Look, you want to go to the ER?"

"I want you to get out of here," said Rick, his voice quiet but slicing. "And turn that frickin' light off."

I took a step back, crossing my arms over my chest. Rick's eyes shifted to me and his mean face fell apart.

"Shit, I'm sorry." His head sank, like his neck was too weak to hold it up. He put his face in his hands.

We all held our places like we'd been playing freeze tag. Sean and Dex in the doorway. Me halfway across the room. Rick on the floor. Then I took a step forward. "Rick?" I said. "Rick, are you hurt?"

His shoulders shook and he made the strangly noise I'd heard on the phone. I turned to the boys and waved them away. Sean took a step back, but Dex stuck. Like Velcro.

"It's okay, you guys. Wait for me outside."

"You sure?" Dex asked.

Rick was all crumpled in on himself, his long legs pulled up close. He didn't have any shoes on, and his bare shins showed between jeans and socks. I couldn't let Sean and Dex stand there and watch him cry. That was wrong.

I turned to Dex and nodded, waving him out the

door.

"Sean and I will be right outside," Dex said loudly. "If you need anything Maxie, just holler. We're not going anywhere."

He flicked off the overhead light and pulled the door almost closed as they left, but didn't let it latch shut.

"You go too," said Rick, muffled through his hands. "Go on. You can't do anything. Nobody can."

"Rick, what happened?"

He shook his head, keeping his face down. I sat across from him, my back against the wall, my knees drawn up like his.

"I'm sorry about the trap," he said, his voice shaking. "I forgot about it. I got everything else, took it home with me, but he was there. He wasn't supposed to get home till Tuesday."

"Who? Your dad?"

He nodded.

"But I'd fucked it all up anyway, the whole thing. The whole goddamn trap. I got there and I couldn't do it."

He started sobbing again, crying like a little kid, with big gulps from deep inside. After one sob he made a hurt-dog yelp. Then he tried to steady his breathing, slow it down. He took a few shaky breaths and looked up.

"You know why?" he asked. His face, the part that wasn't bruised, was flaming red. He wiped his nose with the back of his hand.

I shook my head no, I didn't know why.

"Because he would've been proud of me for it."
Rick's words were muffled and thick like he was talking
through a mouthful of pudding. "One friggin' time in
my whole life, that's what he would've been proud of.
He'd never admit it, but it's true."

Rick sobbed again, winced, and put his face back in
his hands, still talking.

"So I'm standing there at Feltz's locker with a pipe
bomb and I heard Dad's voice in the middle of my head,
loud and clear. 'The little faggot had some guts after
all.' At first I thought yeah, fuck you. Then I sat down
right there and started bawling in the hallway. Cause
the little faggot really doesn't have any guts after all."

The minute he said the words "pipe bomb," all of
my vague fears and maybe-worries spun out of their
misty swirl and locked into place with a sick clunk.
Mousetraps and power failures and iodine reactions.
New Year's resolutions and laser eyes and car doors.
Me, scared off by a mean voice mail. Too scared to
know anything or say anything or do anything.

He went on sobbing like he was never going to quit.
I was still scared but I couldn't pretend I didn't know
what was going on. Not now. I scooted forward a few
inches and put my hand on his foot.

Like the day on the couch when I'd put my hand on
his shoulder, I felt something. A traveling shock wave.
A connection. He took a deep, shuddery breath.

"So now my secret's out," he said, looking up at
me, his acne standing out in red blotches. "I'm a total
nutter. I was going to pull a Columbine. Last week a

bunch of freshmen ganged up on a little fat kid and I decided that was it, it was time."

I shook my head, keeping my eyes locked in with his.

He nodded. "Yup, I had it all set. But you know what?"

I shook my head again.

"Once I thought about that—my dad being proud of me—everything fell apart. Like those freshmen kids, I didn't have their locker numbers. What am I going to do, kill them all? Kill some sixth-grader who maybe threw someone's homework in the toilet this week?"

He tipped his head back, looking at the ceiling.

"It's like I said to you that day, you club one dog down and a thousand more rise to take its place. I thought if I had a big enough club—take out a whole pack of them at once... but then I couldn't."

"But that's good," I said, squeezing his foot.

"Ha. I turned tail and ran home and guess who's standing there? First guy who ever called me a faggot, that's who, in a drunk rage, waiting since midnight. He opened the back of the Explorer and found the pipe bombs and went batshit."

"God, Rick. What'd you do?"

"What'd I do?" he half laughed, then winced and grabbed his side. "What any good little faggot would do, I curled up in a ball on the garage floor while he kicked the shit out of me. I think he broke some ribs, it hurts like hell to breathe."

"Rick, you've got to go to a doctor. Let us take you."

He shook his head.

"He gave me a hundred dollars and the Explorer and told me to get the hell out and never come back. Now I don't know what to do." His voice trembled again and his lower lip shook. "I was going to blow myself away too. I thought I'd be dead this morning."

He dropped his head again and squeezed it between his hands.

"Couldn't even set off my own damn trap. Couldn't even catch myself."

"Shh," I said, rocking his foot.

"If I had any guts I wouldn't be here," he said. "I should've driven off the freeway on the way here but I'm too much of a coward, I'm too..."

"Shhh."

He went back to crying, softer now but on and on, and I kept my hand on his foot, trying to figure out what to do. When Rick finally lifted his head again, his black eye was almost swollen shut, but the other one was wide and wet and crystal green.

"What are you going to do with me?" he asked and I swear he was no more than ten years old, which made it easy.

"I'm going to call Sean and Dex in here to help."

He started shaking his head as soon as I said their names.

"You can't just stay here. You need to get to a doctor. Besides, you and Sean used to be friends, remember?"

"Sean was friends with Roddy," he said. "And Roddy is long gone. Trust me on that."

"Rick, I don't know what else to do. I can't leave you here like this."

"Great. I've screwed things up so bad we have to call in the faggot patrol."

"Rick!" Now I was mad. "Where do you get off calling them faggots? Sean's my cousin, remember? And if it wasn't for Dex I wouldn't even be here right now, he's the one who said I should come. What's the matter with you?"

Rick blinked hard and flinched, like I'd just woken him up with a smack across the face. We looked at each other for a long moment before he spoke.

"More than you can possibly imagine. Go ahead. Call them in."

CHAPTER 22

Rick completely clammed up when Sean and Dex came in the room, just sat there while I told them the basics. Sean called Uncle Max and ran it down to him, and Max said he'd meet us at their house.

Rick didn't say a word until Sean hung up and told him that the Unks both volunteered at Club 99 and had lots of experience working with runaways and kicked-out kids.

Then he snapped his head forward, eyes cold. "That club's for gay kids. I'm not gay."

"Listen Rick," Dex said. "No one here gives a damn if you're gay or not. We're not dragging you off to the club, Sean's just saying these guys have dealt with this kind of family stuff before, all right? You need help, they can help."

"Great," Rick said, tipping his head back to talk to the ceiling. "Club 99, whatever."

After that, it was like all of his lights went out. No tears, no laser looks, nothing. We got him in the back of Dexter's car, and he stared at his feet the whole way. None of us said anything. I could have kissed Dexter when he finally put in a CD, I was so relieved to have something to drown out the silence.

When we pulled into the driveway and Uncle Max stepped out the front door, I'd never been happier to see a real live responsible adult. He asked Rick for his keys and then handed them to Sean.

"Go back to the motel," he said. "Clean out the room, check him out and pay—here's some cash—bring the car back and put it in the garage, door down. Then get back to school. Maxie, you're coming with us."

Sean and Dex left, and I rode with Uncle Max and Rick to urgent care. Uncle Max called Mom on the way to tell her I wasn't in school and why, and could someone pick me up at his house later. He knew what to do about everything. When did that part of being an adult kick in? Sean was over eighteen, but he'd looked as relieved as I'd felt when Max took over and told us all what to do.

I sat alone in the urgent-care waiting room. I crossed my arms over my chest and closed my eyes. My mind buzzed in random directions, going nowhere, figuring out nothing.

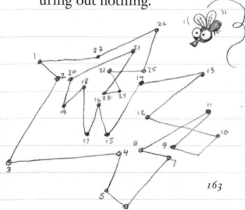

Seemed like a long time before Uncle Max came out, and then even longer before Rick came. He had two broken ribs. They'd taped him up and told him to keep ice packs on his face. Nothing was broken there. We stopped at a pharmacy for pain drugs, and Max ran in. Rick leaned his head against the window with a quiet groan.

"Rick, are you okay?" I asked from the backseat.

"You sound like a broken record," he said. "I'm not okay. Stop asking."

Like slamming full-tilt into a wall of ice.

"Sorry," I said.

When we got back to the house, I waited in the living room while Uncle Max took Rick upstairs to the spare bedroom. I lay on the couch, straining to hear words in the low murmur of voices from upstairs. Max came back down after about fifteen minutes and called Uncle Greg for the fourth time that morning. He said that Rick had taken medication and was going to sleep.

"When can you get here?" he asked Greg. "No, that's fine. I'll have Maxie stay until then."

"Do you mind staying a little while longer?" he asked me after he hung up. "Greg can't get here until two and I have an afternoon class to teach. I don't think Rick will wake up, but just in case. Someone should be here."

"Sure," I said. "I'll call my dad."

Then Uncle Max left and I collapsed again on the couch, exhausted. I closed my eyes and when I opened them, Dad was kneeling beside the couch.

"Maxie? Come on baby, wake up."

I sat up and latched onto him with everything in me. My own parent there, not worried about anyone but me. He wrapped me up in safe daddy arms, my face pressed against the zipper of his down jacket. He stroked my hair and rocked me back and forth a little and I held on tight.

"Sounds like you've had quite a morning," he said.

I nodded.

"You ready to go home?"

"We have to wait till Uncle Greg comes," I said into his jacket.

"He pulled up right behind me," said Dad. "See, there's the garage door now."

We turned Rick over to Greg, and Dad took me home.

I met Sean and Dexter in the Commons at school the next morning.

"How's he doing?" I asked.

"Not like I'd know," said Sean. "He doesn't want any part of me. The Unks are in high gear though. Uncle Max has a therapist lined up for him, and he's got a lawyer friend calling the Youth Law Project to find out about emancipation from his parents."

Tay came in and of course she wanted to know what was going on. I told her Rick got beat up by his dad, leaving out anything about pipe bombs or mousetraps or kisses gone wrong. Then I went up to my locker alone and opened it.

The sprung mousetrap was still on the top shelf where I'd left it. I picked it up by one corner and put it in the inside pocket of my backpack that I never used. I didn't like it—didn't matter that it was sprung, I still felt like it was going to bite me.

I unfolded the picture of Rick. I wished I'd never folded it—it had a crease mark now. That picture was the best thing I'd ever drawn. Looking close, I could see everything in his eyes, beginning to end. From Roddy's first mousetraps all the way to Rick in the hall with a pipe bomb in his hands, and lots of things in between. The good things about Rick and the things that scared me, too. I folded the picture gently back over and slipped it inside my chemistry book.

I'd started moving my books back up on the shelf when I heard Lance's voice.

". . . and then I told him, who cares, I'm already accepted at Duke, I could flunk and who cares and besides, I'm not going to flunk, it's just a stupid—"

I stepped out from my locker row and stood right in front of him. He and Jordan almost mowed me over. They split and went on either side of me.

"—C+, it's not like it's going to make any difference to anyone."

He leaned on the wall and kept talking while Jordan opened his locker, putting his books inside. I stood at the end of the row with my arms crossed, watching them. They didn't look at me; they didn't even notice me standing there.

I could tell them they were lucky they weren't dead. I could tell them exactly what almost happened to them, but what good would it do? Like Rick said, what was I going to do? Threaten everyone? What difference would it make?

CHAPTER 23

I called Uncle Max the next day.

"How long do you think it'll be before Rick comes back to school?" I asked.

There was a long pause on the phone, and then Uncle Max gave a kind of a snort-laugh.

"Maxie. My namesake, my dear one. Did you forget that he almost annihilated that school two days ago?"

"No, I just..."

"He's not going back to that school. We're working on a different placement."

"Oh," I said, feeling young and stupid. "How's he doing?"

Uncle Max sighed.

"He's not that good, actually. His ribs hurt like hell and his face is turning some unbelievably ugly shades of yellow. He's wrecked. Inside and out."

"Should I come over and see him?"

"Mmm, he's got a lot to handle right now. I'll call

you back and let you know."

"Okay," I said.

"You?" he asked. "How are you doing?"

"Oh, I'm fine. Just, you know, worried about Rick."

"You did a great job, getting him some help. I'm proud of you."

I thanked him and we hung up. Proud of me? I wasn't proud of me. *When's he coming back to school?* What was I, ten?

Bad things didn't happen to me. They happened in the McGinnis family—unavoidable with that many people—but not up close where I could really feel them. I not only had white privilege, I had good-parents privilege and no-divorce privilege and safe-home privilege and probably lots of other kinds I hadn't thought of yet.

This time, though, my cushy little safe zone had been touched. Not just touched but smacked around a bit. Now I was trying to get things back to normal so I could feel safe again.

What about Rick, though? He'd stepped completely away from normal. We all ran along on our daily diagrams, this to that to the next, down the slide and up the ladder and swing to the next thing. Maybe a detour here or a choice in direction there, but still the same extended trap. Not Rick. He'd jumped completely off his own page.

Uncle Max called on Saturday and said I could come by and see Rick if I wanted. So Sunday afternoon I took the bus over, and Rick let me in.

"Where is everyone?" I asked.

"Greg's at the garage. Max went shopping. Sean, who knows? They've decided it's safe to leave me alone now."

He wouldn't make eye contact with me. He backed into the house and sat stiffly on the couch.

"How are your ribs?" I asked, sitting in the recliner across from him.

"They hurt," he said.

"Oh. Your face looks better."

"I guess that means you prefer puke yellow and snot green over purple and black."

My tongue sat like dead weight in my mouth.

"So," he said. "Have you drawn a tidy version of my latest mousetrap?"

His mouth twisted up to the side, his eyes cold.

"Mm, no, not your thing," he answered himself. "A little heavy on the realism."

The silence weighed down, pushing me into the chair and making it hard to breathe. The only sound was a clock ticking in the kitchen. I picked at a hangnail, thinking I probably shouldn't have come.

"You know," he said, in a croaky voice. "I hope you're not sitting there thinking you have to visit me. You don't. You don't owe me anything."

"I don't think that. I just wanted to..."

"You don't get to take credit, you know." He sat up straighter, and a tinge of red spread across the tips of his ears. "I started planning the whole thing a long time ago, when I found out we were moving back here."

He didn't look at me. Hadn't since I walked in the door.

"All you did was put the plan on pause for a few minutes." His words sliced, precise and cold. "Until I clued in about your pity-the-poor-Rick game."

"It wasn't a pity game," I said. "That's not what it was at all. That time we spent together, in the snow and stuff, that was, it was . . . that was really fun."

"Great," he said, cutting off my stumbly words at the knees. "So playing in the snow was fun for you, huh? That's just great. Sitting in chemistry next to you every day and knowing I could never touch you, never be close to you, it was like swallowing kerosene. After that day, I let myself think maybe things could be different. I almost believed it until you laughed in my face and said you felt sorry for me. Do you know what that felt like?"

He looked right at me then, glared at me, and whammed his forehead with the heel of his hand, hard, showing me. I felt that blow right between my own eyes. I'd hurt him like that. Me. The room went foggy and wet.

"I'm sorry." I hated my own words, weak and watery and worthless.

"I told you, I don't need your pity."

His ears blazed red and his voice shook and his eyes glowed mean green, shining a spotlight to expose the gutless garbage that I was. Tears chased each other down my cheeks like they couldn't empty out fast enough.

"It's *not* pity!" I said, my voice cracking open. "I'm sorry about *me*. Like how I quit being your friend in sixth grade just because Felicia Sorenson called me a fag hag . . . that scared me. I didn't want to get picked on that way."

"Must've been nice to have a choice."

His voice was like a whip lashing across the room at me, slicing open those stinky bubbling places deep inside that I tried not to think about.

"I know," I said. "I was pathetic and wrong and a big fat chicken and I hate that. I didn't even think about you, I only thought about me. But that time we spent together, it wasn't because I felt sorry for you. I know that's what you thought I was saying, but it wasn't, not like you think."

His jaw was locked down tight, teeth clenched, face blazing, eyes narrow. As I spoke, a tremble moved across his face, eased his eyebrows up and touched his lower lip. He sucked some air, swallowed, and clenched down again. Seeing that pain and how hard he was working not to show it touched me deeper than watching him sob in the motel.

"That day when we kissed, Rick, I don't know exactly what happened. I mean, it happened before I really knew what was going on and then, then, then it was too fast and it freaked me out, I wasn't ready for all that."

I stopped and caught my breath, wiped my face and sniffed hard. The clock ticked, pushing me to say more.

"I liked kissing you, okay? I did. I haven't even had

five seconds to think about that because then everything went so bad so fast. I don't know what I'm supposed to say or do now but the way I feel about you, it's not pity. It's, I don't know. Complicated."

"You know what a fool I felt like?" he blurted. "Having you come and scrape me up off the floor of a Motel 6? The person I most want to see me as something, anything other than what I really am."

"No, don't say that. What you are is good."

He snorted, rolling his eyes sideways.

"I love who you are."

The last sentence hung free in the air between us, and it was true. I couldn't look at him anymore. I couldn't look at anything but my own hands, twitching and fidgeting in my lap.

In a teen movie world, this was the time for music to swell and credits to roll. But in real life, we sat there shaky and messy with our hearts hanging out in the wind.

The clock continued ticking like it was stepping toward us with each twitch of the second hand.

"I'm gonna get a gun and shoot that frickin' clock," said Rick, and I laughed, letting out the breath I'd been holding.

"How can they stand it?" I asked.

"I don't know. I can even hear it upstairs. I'm

tempted to throw it in the river."

We both laughed a little and breathed a little.

"You going to stay here much longer?" I asked.

"I don't know," he shrugged. "I saw a shrink a couple of times this week, he thinks I should stick for a while. Not like I have anyplace else to go."

"I bet you're getting some good food at least," I said.

"Food, that part is beyond belief. Greg is the original gourmet mechanic."

The garage door rumbled.

"That's Max," said Rick.

We both stood up and kind of shuffled around. Rick cleared his throat, and I wiped my face again and wished I had a Kleenex. I glanced at Rick's face, then back at the floor, then made myself meet his eyes. They were the clear green glass that I'd seen out in the snow, at the coffee shop, on the couch in my own living room. He bobbed his head, gave me a half smile, and headed for the stairs.

CHAPTER 24

The next few days I went through the motions of my life, school and homework, lunch with Tay or Dexter, but I wasn't even halfway there. I kept thinking about the old Nash & Hawke, Ink traps. They all had gaps— places where the mouse could slip away. Rick's real-life trap was a direct path to blowing up lockers and maybe killing someone, and he escaped—slid off the page just before he hit the boom-point.

But where, exactly, did that trap start?

What if we'd gone to a different middle school, what if there'd been no Felicia to call me names, or even if she had, what if I hadn't dumped Rod in sixth grade? What if he'd been in a different P.E. class, what if the gym teacher had stayed in the locker room that day, what if Sean hadn't shown up when he did and run for help? Or what about all the things that happened to Rick between seventh grade and the first day of chemistry, things I knew nothing about? Everything starts somewhere, but how do you figure where?

It was like trying to trace one of our old mousetraps back to the first bite of cheese. If you could just remove the piece of cheese from that spot, the end of the trap would never snap.

But what if you could recognize a bad run somewhere in the middle, before things started dropping on your head? Could you step sideways, or even spin and scoot in a totally different direction?

On Wednesday, I tracked Tay down after last period.

"What are you doing now?" I asked.

"Nothing, I guess. Why?"

"Want to walk with me?" I asked. "I can get my dad to take you home later."

She stood with one hand on her locker door, looking at me. I met her eyes and held them. It was the first time I'd done that in a long, long time. She nodded, and we walked outside together.

It had been cool on the way to school in the morning, but things had been heating up all afternoon. We stepped out into a drippy, wet, water-running, warm-breeze-blowing first day of spring. The sun beat down on the few piles of snow clinging to the edges of the parking lot and squeezed out the last bits of cold. The melting chunks of ice dripped and trickled to the gutter, where they joined the sounds of winter gurgling down the storm drains and out to the river. The dead yellow

175

grass perked up and thought about being green again.

On the front lawn several hacky circles were gathered, kids flicking limbs around to the beat of a boom box on the sidewalk. Footballs and frisbees flew, and three skaters clattered by in front of us. We turned left toward my house and walked a few blocks in silence, side by side, hands in pockets. The wind lifted my hair and set it back down again, airing out my brain.

My heart started to thud faster as I worked myself up to talk. Cars swooshed by on the wet pavement, bass pulsing from the speakers.

"Are we still friends?" I asked.

"I don't know," Tay answered quickly. "Are we?"

We stopped on the curb, waiting to cross the street. A blue Mustang went by, windows open and music blaring. Its tires spattered water and we stepped back.

"I'm sorry about the glass," I said.

"What grass?"

"Glass. As in, glass door. Remember, on my birthday? How I wouldn't let you in?"

We crossed the street and kept walking.

"Yeah, I remember all right," said Tay, setting her chin.

"I'm sorry. Sorry I did that."

"You had a right to be mad about your birthday," she said, walking faster. I sped up to keep pace. "It's just that you wouldn't let it go. Like nothing I could do was going to make any difference."

"Maybe I thought it wouldn't matter to you," I said. "Like the day I went snowboarding with you, you had a lot more fun without me. Guess I figured it was just going to be like that."

I glanced sideways at her. She had her eyes on the ground, eyebrows drawn together. It was the thinking-Tay face. I'd seen it lots of times.

"You swooshing off down the hill with the cool people and me sitting on my butt in the snow, hoping maybe you'll—"

"Maxie, you're my best friend," she cut me off and stopped to face me. "So you don't snowboard, so what? You didn't play hockey either."

I took a deep breath and kept going.

"I'm scared about the drugs," I said. "And that I'm not cool enough for you anymore. I mean, I actually kissed Rick Nash. How's that for not cool?"

"Nash?" her eyes went wide, her eyebrows shooting up under her hair. "Roddy, Rick Nash?"

"See?" I said, nodding. "Really not cool." I turned and started walking again, and we crossed the street over to the edge of the park. "Tay, people die from doing drugs. I know, everyone says not me, I'm careful. But then some of them die anyway."

"Maxie," she said, and I felt her make the effort not to roll her eyes. "I'm not going to die from smoking a little weed."

"What about the E?" I asked.

"That," she said, flicking it away with her fingers. "I know, that's maybe kinda stupid. I don't do it that often. Especially not since the snow's gone."

It wasn't all gone. Piles of it still hunched around

where the ice rink used to be, but they were going down so fast you could almost see them shrinking.

"So what, when it snows again you're going to start doing it more? Why do you want to do it at all?"

"See? If I even talk about any of this to you, you start looking at me like I'm some kind of drug scum."

"It's not that," I said. "It scares me. When you're high, it's like you're not there anymore. I don't like that."

The asphalt walk cut across the middle of the park. The grass was a mess of mud and huge icy puddles. Some elementary school kids ran back and forth on the wet tennis court, smacking their feet and splashing each other and squealing and laughing.

"I guess that's what I like about it," she said. "When I'm high, it's like I'm not here anymore."

"Is it that bad here?"

A cardinal swooped onto a tree branch ahead, lifted its little red chin up and started hollering for all it was worth. "Wha-cheer, cheer, cheer." Like it knew how pretty it was against that burning blue sky and wanted everyone to stop and look.

We did, tipping our heads back and watching until it flew, bobbing and dipping in the air to a tree on the other side of the park. Then Tay turned to me and said, "Only sometimes."

We started walking again. Nervous jitters wiggled through me. My teeth would have chattered if I hadn't held them still.

"What if I say I won't smoke around you?" said

Tay. "Will you take the glass down and hang out with me sometimes and talk about something besides stupid schoolwork?"

I watched our feet, my clean brown shoes and her raggedy hightops, stepping along together on the asphalt. I'd missed Tay so much, and not just because I didn't have anyone to do things with. I'd missed her broad bold strokes of feeling and excitement, the shifting clouds of her moods, the way she could shake me loose and make me laugh even when I didn't want to.

"Yeah, I can take the glass down. But it'll be weird if you just don't smoke around me, like I'm a cop or something. I'll always be thinking you wish I wasn't there so you could do what you want."

"You've been not there so I could do what I want and I didn't like it," said Tay, kicking a chunk of ice so it skittered ahead of us. "But I can't promise you I'll quit, then I'd end up sneaking and lying."

"Don't sneak and lie. I hate that."

"Don't judge me. I hate that."

I sighed big. "Why can't you just do what I want you to?"

Tay laughed and it sounded so good. I hadn't heard her laugh in a long time.

"I'll do what you want sometimes and the rest of the time I'll try not to be a jerk. How's that?"

"Better than no Tay," I said. "No Tay was bad."

"That's right," she leaned over and bumped me with her shoulder. "Now what's the deal with you and Nash?"

"Mmm, long story. I mean, really *really* long story."

I took the left fork of asphalt, the one that cut across where the ice rink had been. Muddy water spread across ahead of us.

"When do I get to hear it? Do you want to get together this weekend? Or are you too busy with your new BOYfriend?"

I jumped into the shallow puddle in front of us, coming down hard with both feet. The water spattered Tay's legs.

"Hey!" she said, breaking into a huge grin. "What's that about?"

She stomped, and drips rained over the front of my jeans. I stepped off the asphalt into the deep muddy puddle, and it seeped icy cold into my shoes. I kicked water at Tay. She jumped in too and we splashed back and forth, kicking and squealing and stomping like five-year-olds. In no time my pants were soaked from the knees down. Bits of muddy grit splashed all the way up on my neck. The sun shone down on us and the warm breeze blew around us and we laughed and hollered things like, "Oh yeah?" and "Take that," and "Oh, I'll get you for that one."

It was the most fun I'd had since shoveling snow.

CHAPTER 25

It worked. Tay and I stepped onto a new page. We still had some bumpy spots, but I didn't duck away from them and neither did she. It was like we'd both been gone for a long time, and now we were getting to know each other again.

It was good to finally tell her about the kiss on the couch.

"Really?" she asked, amazed. "Rick Nash is a good kisser?"

"For a minute he was," I said. "Then, I don't know. He wasn't. Or I wasn't."

"Do you want to kiss him again?"

Dexter had asked me that about thirty-seven startling events ago.

"I don't know," I said, as Tay drained her soda. "Yes and no."

"Huh. Maybe that's just how it is. I kissed Sam one night at a party and it was great, but then the next time it wasn't great at all and now I think we've stopped kissing.

Why isn't it like in the movies?"

"Nothing is," I said. "Unless you're Sean and Dex."

"How ironic is that?" laughed Tay.

I called Rick that night and asked for help on my chemistry homework, and he walked me through it.

"How's the new school?" I asked him, once we got chemistry out of the way.

"It's full of druggies and sexual deviants and hostile life forms. I fit right in."

It was the first time I'd talked to him since our big clock-ticking conversation, and I wasn't sure what else to say. I guess he wasn't either, because after a few seconds of silence he said, "Hey, my battery's low, I should hang up."

I started to call him a few times after that, but then didn't. I kept thinking he'd call me, but he didn't.

A couple of weeks later I was at Target looking for a birthday present for Dad. I came around the end of an aisle and spotted Rick. He was in the DVD section talking to a medium-fat girl with long blonde hair and a sharp pointy face. She said something and he cracked up, laughing so hard he could barely stand.

My stomach did a jump and spin and I stepped to the next aisle. I knew I should just walk over and say hi, but if I did, I'd wreck the laugh. It'd be awkward, and I'd feel stupid and wish I hadn't done it, so I just didn't.

When I got home, I picked the picture of Rick up off my dresser. I'd had it there, face down, since the day after the trap snapped. It had been too intense to look at, all those different green-eyed Ricks packed into one picture with a crease mark across his face.

What was I to him now? Just another hard-wired hazard in the trap he'd managed to escape? What about my trap?

Ladders to chutes, keeping my mouth shut, putting up glass doors, stepping away, on down the page.

I picked up the phone and called Sean.

He came out to the Grands' the next day, without Dexter, because I told him I'd kill him if he didn't.

"All right, all right," he said, getting out of his car. "I'm here. Thank you for the lecture on family obligations. Is there anything else I've been slipping up on?"

"Yes," I said, leading him down the drive. "Me. You owe me for six months of neglect. Since October it's been all about Dexter and we've hardly talked. I still can't believe you knew less about what was going on with me and Rick than Dexter did. That's wrong."

"Hey, it's not my fault you didn't bother to tell me. Anyway, I was there for you that day, wasn't I?"

"Defensive!" I yelled.

"Okay, okay," he said. "Maybe I haven't been exactly available. I've just been busy, you know?"

"I know. Busy with Dexter. I know more about what's up with you guys from him than I do from you."

We walked under the oaks, then turned to follow the fence line along the field. The new grass was springy underfoot. "Now I'm going to give you a chance to make up for it. Is Rick going out with anyone?"

"What?" he turned to face me.

"Going out with anyone. Rick. Is he?"

"He doesn't exactly confide in me, you know. I hardly even see him since he started working at the garage with Greg."

"Working? Rick?"

"Yeah, he's working weekends and a couple of evenings, even though they told him he didn't have to pay rent, and how fair is that, they told me I do have to start paying rent after I graduate and I'm their own flesh and blood. Anyway, I'm moving to campus. I'm trying to talk Dexter into moving in with me, and I think maybe he will, his mom's really been working on his dad and they—"

"Sean!" I yelled it loud, and he clapped both hands over his mouth, his eyes smiling.

"So why are you asking?" he said, taking his hands away. "You're not..."

"I saw him with this girl in Target and I was, I don't know, just wondering."

I scanned the trees along the edge of the field. Tiny buds put a breath of light green on the bare branches.

"I never realized it before," he said, "but when you blush, your freckles sort of disappear. It's like they get swallowed up into the red. It's kinda cool, really."

"Shut up."

"Do you really like him that way? I mean, he's not exactly, you know. Stable."

"I know, but he's getting more stable, right? Maybe I could help."

"I'm not sure signing up to be his girlfriend is the way to do it."

"I'm not signing up for anything," I said. "I'm just asking."

"So did you really call me out here to see the Grands, or just to pump me for information about Rick?"

"Come on," I said, grabbing his elbow and turning him back toward the house. "They probably forgot what you look like. Don't forget to call Grandpa 'sir,' he'll like you better that way."

Sean put his arm around my shoulders while we walked back. Just before we got to the front sidewalk, he said, "I'll nose around and see what I can find out about the Target babe. But I think you should be careful about casting out those hot McGinnis vibes. No one can resist us, you know."

I punched him in the stomach, and we went inside.

A little over a week later, Rick waited for me at the park after school. I came around the corner and there he was, right on time, sitting at the picnic table. A couple of kids played basketball on the court behind him. The sky hung gray and hot and low, holding back a rainstorm.

"Thanks for coming," I said as I walked up.

"No problem. Looks like we might get rained out, though."

I set my backpack down, unzipped it, pulled out a package wrapped in Mighty Mouse paper, and handed it to him.

"It's for you," I said. "I wanted it to be better."

He turned it over, sliding a finger under the paper to loosen the tape.

"Vintage wrapping paper. Nice choice."

I held my breath as he turned it over and pulled the paper away.

"Huh," he said. "Look at that."

The cartoon strip I had sweat blood over was inset in a frame beneath my original, still-creased drawing of Rick. He pulled it closer, drawing his brows together as he studied the cartoon. I bit my lip. Maybe it was stupid.

"Superhero, huh? That's got to be the most creative spin in history. You even put a formula in, I'm proud of you."

"Do you like it? I wanted it to be a lot better."

"Yeah, I like it," he said. "Reminds of something too. You know that thing your parents say about moral fiber? They're right. That's what really kept me from blowing everything away. Shoveling snow. Tell your parents that, okay? I think they'll like it."

"Sure," I said, swallowing hard.

So that December day had jimmied a connection loose in Rick's trap, a gap that stuck even after everything else went wrong. Long before he'd stood in the hall with a pipe bomb in his hands and thought about his dad, clearing the walks had started something that ended something. Or ended something that started something.

He looked at the picture. I looked at him looking at the picture. My pulse started thumping in my ears so hard it almost rocked my head back and forth.

"So," I said.

He glanced up, met my eyes, and put the picture down. He folded his hands on the table again and waited. The sky waited, full of possibility. Even I waited.

"So," I said again. I was stuck there.

One fat raindrop splashed on the table between us. Rick pulled the wrapping paper back around the picture and held it on his lap with his arms around it. He looked up at the sky. Another drip came down and hit him on the forehead. He wiped it off.

"So...?"

"So, ah. I was wondering."

A few more raindrops smattered on the table, soaking into the thirsty wood. It needed a paint job.

"Better wonder faster or we're going to get wet," said Rick, moving to get up.

"Wait," I said.

The rain whispered across the grass. The kids left the basketball court and ran off down the street. Rick settled back onto the bench, hunched over the picture to protect it.

"Do you want to go out on a date sometime?" I finally got it out in a rush, splatting onto the table with the raindrops.

"With you?" asked Rick.

"Um, yeah."

"Come on," he said, standing up. "Let's get in my car so this doesn't get wet."

He ran for the Explorer, long legs flying, and got in. I sat in the rain with his non-answer until he pushed the passenger door open and honked the horn. Then I trudged over and got in, pushing my wet hair back off my forehead.

"Maxie, why did you ask me that?" Rick asked as soon as I shut the door.

On the walk over, I'd been hoping we'd both pretend like I hadn't asked. I closed my eyes and reached inside, past the ego-poke of getting turned down by Rick Nash, past my embarrassment.

"It's true what I said," I said over the raindrops slapping the windshield. "That Sunday over at the Unks. About how I feel about you."

Long, long silence. Longer than six solid pages of busy mousetraps. Only the rain moved, banging on the roof like it was trying to get in. Then, suddenly, it eased off as if someone had just called its name, pulled it in another direction.

"If you'd said this a couple of months ago I'd be on top of the world," Rick said quietly. "But after everything..." he shifted in his seat, turning to face me. "Maxie, I'm kind of a nutter."

"So?" I said. "It's not like I've got everything together."

Rick shifted again, faced the fogging windshield, and grabbed the top of the steering wheel with both hands.

"You don't get it, do you?"

"Get what?"

"I've got a long ways to go before I can think about having a girlfriend, especially you. Because you know what? It wouldn't work, and then you'd feel guilty and I'd feel like a pile of steaming shit, and I'd never see you again."

"How do you know it wouldn't work?" I asked.

"I can tell," he said quietly. "You don't feel like me like I do about you, I can tell by the way you look at me."

That's the same thing Dexter had said earlier at lunch when I'd told him I was going to ask Rick out. He'd said I didn't feel the same and it wasn't fair, but I figured he thought I was too shallow to like someone like Rick, or too much of a coward to stick in there if it got hard. I wanted to prove them both wrong, show that I was a good person, a really good loyal person who wasn't worried about what people thought. I did love Rick, I really did. I just needed to give things a fair chance.

"But if we go slow," I said. "And give it some time. I mean, I really like you, Rick. I do."

"Then forget the date thing, okay?"

He had just enough of the laser-eyes tone in that last sentence that I looked up. He was staring, hard, at the dashboard.

"I can't believe I'm saying this, but I mean it. Max, will you just be my goddamn friend? That's what I need."

I hated myself for the rush of relief I felt as Rick took a big breath, blew it out, and said, "And that's what I want."

"Really?" I asked in a small voice.

"Really. Can you do that?"

I didn't want to answer right away. Because if I said yes to this, then I had to mean it. For real. No matter what the Felicias or the canaille or anyone else had to say.

Rick started the engine and lowered all the windows. The last drops of rain had spattered down the street and off to the west and a light breeze blew in, chasing away the fog on the glass. I still didn't say anything. There were a lot of Ricks inside Rick, and some of them I didn't like. But there were a lot of Tays, too, including the stoned one, and somehow I'd figured out how to be friends with all of her.

"So maybe you can't," he said, and his voice walked the edge of a tight shaky line as he put the car in gear. "That's okay. We do what we can, right?"

He pulled away from the curb. A patch of blue broke through the clouds out my window and the sun shot streams of light through the dripping trees along the boulevard.

"I can," I said, and as soon as it fell out of my mouth I knew it was true.

We turned onto my street, and Rick pulled up in front of my house.

"Really?" he asked, turning to me, and Roddy's eyes rode on his question.

"Yes," I said, and my voice got bigger. "I can."

He smiled with both sides of his mouth and gave me his special little head-bob. I unbuckled my seat belt and smiled back at him.

"See you later then?" he said.

"Not too much later, okay?" I said as I got out.

He bobbed again and drove off. I stood on the front stoop and watched the Explorer turn right at the stop sign and disappear. I looked across the snowless green yard. The sidewalk was bare, but I could hear and see half an echo of Rick and Maxie on that frigid sunshine morning, clearing the concrete and amping up our moral fiber. My own words, those simple ones—*yes* and *I can*, I tasted them and felt them move up from my guts through my heart, across my lips and into the air.

Everything starts somewhere and everything ends somewhere, and mostly you don't know which one is when. But sometimes, you do.

ABOUT THE AUTHOR

Pat Schmatz is the author of *Circle the Truth*, which *Kirkus Reviews* called "an unusual and valuable addition to the pantheon of literature" for teen readers. Over the years, she has supported her writing habit with a variety of jobs, including forklift operator, janitor, fitness consultant, stable hand, secretary, and shipping clerk. Ms. Schmatz grew up in rural Wisconsin and still lives in the woods of her childhood.